CHEERLEADERS

#30

SAYING YES

CAROLINE B. COONEY

SCHOLASTIC INC.
New York Toronto London Auckland Sydney

No part of this publication may be reproduced in whole or in part, or stored in a retrieval system, or transmitted in any form or by any means, electronic, mechanical, photocopying, recording, or otherwise, without written permission of the publisher. For information regarding permission, write to Scholastic Inc., 730 Broadway, New York, NY 10003.

ISBN 0-590-40635-3

12 11 10 9 8 7 6 5 4 3 2 1   7 8 9/8 0 1 2/9

Printed in the U.S.A   01

First Scholastic printing, June 1987

CHEERLEADERS

SAYING YES

CHEERLEADERS

CHAPTER

The plane slid through cloudy skies, halfway between New York City and Tarenton. The two passengers in 41A and B were still in a state of shock at finding each other on the same plane. They were holding hands, half in delight, half in confusion.

And Pres Tilford, for lack of anything else to say, flashed a wide grin at the lovely golden-haired girl next to him. "If we can't think of anything else to do once we're back in Tarenton," he said softly, "we could always get married."

Mary Ellen Kirkwood fixed him with her most scathing look. *If we can't think of anything else to do!* she thought. *How romantic of him.* "I ought to toss you out of the plane for that, Pres."

"Have a heart. We're a mile high."

"Perfect. Just what you deserve."

Pres kept right on holding her hand. "But Melon, I thought you were always crazy about me."

"Always was . . . intrigued by you. Still am. Probably will be forever. But the man who marries me will propose *right*."

When they were Varsity Cheerleaders together at Tarenton High, she would have blown up if Pres called her Melon. She'd wanted *Mary Ellen* to become a household word: model, cover girl, television actress, talk-show hostess. Now she blushed to remember all her wild daydreams. How shocked she had been to find that the sidewalks of New York were covered with lovely, slender, blonde models from the Midwest.

She waitressed at various restaurants and coffeehouses. She rushed frantically to appointments that led to little or nothing. Her portfolio grew, but slowly. Mary Ellen had expected money, lovely clothing, jewelry, status — and most of all, fun.

Fun was sadly lacking in New York.

To have fun, you needed cash. Nobody Mary Ellen met could earn enough. She shared a tiny apartment with three other hopeful models. Mary Ellen never dreamed she would be that poor again — she who had even once done laundry in high school to earn the money to buy herself clothing.

Going home, she thought, staring out the plane window into the gray mist. How will it feel to come home? Eventually I'm going to have to

2

admit that the great Mary Ellen turned out to be ordinary.

Mary Ellen touched her golden hair. Her year in the city had taught her, if nothing else, precisely how to fix it. Sometimes she could toss off her dreary thoughts simply by touching her hair, and this time it worked like a charm. Now she could turn to Pres and beam at him. What a wonderful, handsome guy he was! She felt the first real yearning to be back home, where things were comfortably familiar.

Pres said, "I propose to you and you want to throw me out of the plane, huh? You'd rather have me splat on a mountainside than wait for you in church?"

Mary Ellen giggled. She and Pres had always been able to talk. All the happiness of their high school years, especially the many hours shared in athletics and cheering, swept over both of them. In a surge of nostalgia, they leaned the few inches between the airline seats and kissed softly.

Mary Ellen pulled away much faster than she expected to. A shiver of emotion ran over her. All her life she had known and envied Pres Tilford. But for many reasons, they had never quite come together in high school. The cheerleading squad that bound them together also kept them apart. "How come you were in New York and didn't call me?" she asked.

Pres did not move back. Staring into her cornflower blue eyes he said, "Business trip, and I wanted to give you some space for a little while."

"Oh, right," Mary Ellen said, laughing. "Are you and Patrick flying people's household goods now? Or did you forget to pack somebody's wrist-watch and have to make a special-delivery trip?"

Patrick had been in love with Mary Ellen in their junior and senior years. Big, strong, self-willed Patrick, as handsome as Pres but much more rugged, had had his own business before he was sixteen, and it had grown into a large and lucrative garbage route. Mary Ellen had never quite been able to overcome the snobbery she felt about dating a boy who picked up garbage, and Patrick had never quite been able to overcome his anger that she judged him like that. Then Patrick had started a moving business with Pres, too.

It was funny. Mary Ellen had flown home months ago to participate in a local fashion show, and she'd run into Patrick. Whatever yearning they had had for each other — emotional, sexual, and visual — had evaporated. Patrick was happily dating one of the new cheerleaders, a girl named Jessica, and Mary Ellen had found herself chatting to him as if to a pleasant neighbor. When she thought of the emotional tangles she and Patrick had gotten themselves into! And now it was gone with the wind.

But Pres was something different. Mary Ellen could not take her eyes off Pres.

Whatever was happening between *them* was definitely *not* gone with the wind. Even as they sat there, she could feel it intensifying. Something in Mary Ellen murmured, Look out. This is real. This is strong. You'd better be ready.

I'm not ready, she thought, and abruptly turned to stare out the window. Nothing there but thick, soggy gray.

"I'm working for Tarenton Fabricators now," Pres said lightly. "I wanted to tell you in person. Can you believe it? After all these years of fighting my father and refusing to have a single thing to do with the family business, last month I started work in the factory. As I told Patrick, I just walked by the buildings one day and I knew that's what I wanted to do. Learn the factory inside out, and Patrick understood. You see, Dad knows only the business angles: office and legal and marketing. He almost never even drives past the factories, let alone sees what's happening there on the lines. And I . . . well, working with Patrick, I got over a lot of my snobbery. I got excited, Melon. I looked at those huge buildings, stretching block after block, filled with hundreds of workers, and I thought, That's what I want — to run that."

Mary Ellen's eyes lit up with pleasure. "Oh, Pres! I think that's wonderful! I'm so proud of you. I never thought you'd make that decision."

"Neither did I," he confessed. "My dad still wishes I'd go to Princeton like he did, but school isn't for me. I can't stand any more of it. But I found out I really like work. And when I started in the factory . . . I sort of . . . well. . . ."

Pres was the one to turn away this time. A

5

slight flush spread on tanned cheeks that never blushed. He had almost said, I fell in love with the factory. But that would have been ridiculous. He would have been so embarrassed to say a thing like that. You didn't fall in love with buildings, with steel, with welding, with assembly lines.

"You sort of what?" Mary Ellen asked. Her voice was softer than he remembered. Mellow. Gentle. How much older she seemed to Pres now. They weren't that long out of high school, and yet how far they had come! "Sort of fell in love with it?" she said.

"How did you know?" he exclaimed.

"I could see it. You look so much happier than I've ever seen you. I'm so happy for you, Pres. I just wish I could say the same about where I am in life."

"Where are you in life?" Pres asked immediately.

She shrugged and laughed, proud of herself for being able to laugh. "Some dreams die hard, Pres. But I had to lay mine to rest. I'm not top-drawer. I'm pretty good, but in New York City, that's not good enough."

His arms went around her for comfort, and Mary Ellen felt the tremendous relief of friendship. The words spilled out of her, telling him the pain, the failure, the frustration, the determination . . . and finally, one agonizing night, hours after she should have been asleep, the realization that it was time to go home and figure out a different plan for her life.

They talked intensely for an hour, discussing

6

where life had led them. "I think," said Mary Ellen, "I'll go to the junior college and take basic liberal arts courses. I just don't know what I want to do now. I need a year to think. And I'll have to get a job." She could think of nothing but waitressing, but that wasn't really so bad. You met a lot of people, had flexible hours, and a relatively good income.

"Actually, Pres," she said suddenly, "I adore babies. I could work at one of the day-care centers in Tarenton."

"You adore babies?" he repeated, stupified. "I would have thought you were the last girl on earth to want to change diapers and pour glasses of juice and teach the alphabet."

"A year ago I wouldn't have admitted it to a soul," she nodded. "I was too . . . oh, I don't know, Pres. I think I was too shallow. I don't feel a year older, I feel a decade older."

He tried to see her running a day-care center. Impossible. "I think going to the junior college and getting an easier part-time job would be a thousand percent better for you," he said.

They were both amazed when the pilot announced that they were to fasten their seat belts because the plane was about to land. Mary Ellen fumbled trying to find the right end, and Pres handed it to her silently. A curious shiver ran up her arm from where his fingers touched her. She thought, Oh, Mary Ellen, you'd better watch your step. No cheerleading fall was ever as complex as the fall you could take over Pres.

The seat belts snapped gently into place. The

7

pilot's voice droned with static. They came lower than the clouds, and the buildings of the regional airport came up at them with frightening speed. The tires hit too hard, and the plane bounced. Mary Ellen stiffened, the way she always did on a plane, not wanting to think of accidents and death, but thinking of them anyway.

"So you'll have to go back to sharing a tiny bedroom and a single closet with your sister Gemma," Pres said, shaking his head. "What a life, Melon. Listen, I think we ought to get married." He put on a wide, insane smile and winked at her with alternate eyelids. It made her laugh. "Come on," he said. "We'll have fun."

"When I get married, it will be forever," Mary Ellen Kirkwood said. The plane stopped. She undid her seat belt.

"I wasn't exactly going to get married for the weekend, either," Pres said.

Mary Ellen shook her head. A joking proposal was almost worse than none at all. Poor — grindingly poor — as the Kirkwoods might be, her parents' marriage was a beautiful thing and Mary Ellen intended to have no less. Her fantasies of marriage were very involved, and very complete. Pres had wealth, and Pres had looks, and Pres definitely excited her, interested her. But he was being silly and she resented it. Right now her life was seriously confused. All her dreams had expired, no new dreams were awaiting her, and whatever happened next would be nothing but painful, humiliating compromise. Mary Ellen didn't want Pres cracking jokes about how they ought to get married.

For one thing, it was ridiculous.

For another, she wouldn't be able to stop herself from daydreaming about it. And that would kill her, because it was just a joke to Pres.

"What's happening in Tarenton?" she asked as they got up to leave the plane. "How's the new squad? Heard from the others? Nancy? Walt? Angie?"

For the first few months of the school year, Pres had hung out at the high school as if he had never graduated. Perhaps he had *not* graduated emotionally. The ties of high school life had been unbroken, and he needed to go to the games, visit old classes, and sit in on cheerleading practices. He and Patrick had both done it. Pres had gotten himself nearly as involved in the new cheerleading squad as in the old.

But that need had dwindled.

He had barely thought of them since he'd begun work at Tarenton Fabricators. "I haven't heard from the old gang, and the new group are all fine, but not one of the girls matches you. You have real style."

They grinned easily at each other.

Pres's family was extremely wealthy, with a magnificent waterfront mansion on Fable Point. Pres had driven a Porsche since the day he got his driver's license, and routinely taken vacations in Europe.

Mary Ellen's family lived (there was no nice

way to put it) in a tiny, surpassingly ugly, turquoise tract house in a whole neighborhood of equally run-down houses.

"You've always had polish, Melon," Pres said, "and you've had style since you walked into kindergarten. You've had poise since you had the lead in the first-grade play."

Oh, how she needed the praise! What a long time it had been since anybody had thought Mary Ellen had style and poise. I hope he asks me for a date, she thought. How much easier to go home knowing I have a date with Pres Tilford for Saturday night.

And then she began laughing helplessly. How absurd that after two proposals of marriage she should be afraid he might not ask her for Saturday!

"What's so funny?" Pres demanded.

She told him, still laughing.

A year ago, in high school, she would *never* have admitted insecurity like that. Now it seemed comical and sure enough Pres thought so, too. "Saturday night," he said. "Well, I don't know. I mean, if we're not going to get married, I'm not sure I want all these demands put on my time."

"It is pretty forward of me," Mary Ellen said. "Premarital dating. Heavy, you know?"

How they laughed.

The laughs were wonderful: strong with friendship . . . and more, and solid with years and years of knowing each other. Crossing the runway, they paused to hug, and hugged again in the terminal.

It won't be so bad after all, Mary Ellen thought, to come home in defeat. I have Pres, at least, and I still have the courage I'm going to need.

In spite of the gloom and the rain, life looked good to Mary Ellen Kirkwood.

As for Pres Tilford, he thought life was looking very mysterious.

I, Pres, actually proposed to a girl, he thought. *Twice.*

I, Pres, who was going to be a swinging bachelor for another decade. I proposed. I guess I'm lucky. She said no.

He stared at the perfect, classic profile beside him. Am I in love with Mary Ellen? he thought. Was that all a joke? Something to say on a plane? Or did I mean it?

Tears had filled Mary Ellen's eyes. Following her gaze he realized it was the sight of a huge wall map, whose arrows showed the driving routes to nearby cities. Tarenton: northeast.

Were they tears of joy that she was home?

Or tears of grief that only failure brought her back?

Probably both, Pres thought. Never in his life had he so much wanted to know the answers. To offer comfort, and affection, and —

Wow, thought Pres, blowing out a lungful of air to calm himself down. Tilford, get a grip on yourself. You're nineteen, remember?

"My Porsche is in the long-term parking lot," he said. "I'll drive you home, sweetheart."

"Thanks, Pres."

11

They went to get her luggage. He had only his carryon bag, but she had a number of suitcases. The Porsche was going to see its first use as a moving van.

And the word *sweetheart* had had its first use, too.

He had never meant it before.

CHAPTER

The same rain that enveloped New York was falling in Tarenton. The cheerleading squad of Tarenton High had finished their daily practice at almost the same moment that Pres and Mary Ellen got into his Porsche. It was the time of year when most people had had enough of bad weather. It was difficult to look forward to bundling up in six layers yet another morning. The rain fell heavily, and without wind, as if the drops were tired and wanted to lie down immediately.

Olivia Evans felt the same.

Okay, she said to herself. Intellectually you know exactly what's going on. You know Diana Tucker is still being her nasty, scheming self, and you know that somehow she's won Tara Armstrong to her cause. That's all it is, Livvy. A sick, unbalanced, jealous girl who wants to be what you are. So overlook it, Livvy.

13

But Olivia could not treat the problem intellectually. The six members of the cheerleading squad were too intensely bound up in each other to remain calm and academic about emotional problems. Here was Diana up to her old tricks, and Olivia wanted to weep, or stomp her foot, or possibly shove her fist through a wall. Or through Diana's face.

At a time like this you needed a girl friend, not a boyfriend. Much as she loved David Duffy, he was a boy. There were moments when only a female friend could understand. And this was one of them.

I can't talk to Hope Chang, Olivia thought, dismissing the fragile, beautiful girl on the squad. Hope's never been close to me. I can't talk to Jessica Armstrong, because I've never gotten all that close to her, either. And certainly not to Tara. She's the whole problem. If Tara had just told Diana to take a long walk off a short dock, I wouldn't have these horrible feelings in the first place. It isn't loyal of Tara to take up with Diana. Here we proved that Diana tried to sabotage our squad. We all know she actually fooled around with Tara's car to keep us from a game, and yet Tara is *still* getting friendly with her! And they're ganging up on me again. I know it, I can feel it.

But to whom could Olivia say this?

Diana was not at the practice. Tara had not said anything definite. Tara hadn't even been a pain. She had worked as hard as the other five.

And yet Olivia knew she was right.

She stared into the thick gray northern sky.

Rain landed on her cheeks and eyelashes. Am I being a pouting little girl? she asked herself. Or a wise adult? Making things up? Or understanding things at last?

If only Mary Ellen was still around!

Olivia's longing for the previous squad — never far from her memory — swept over her yet again. How perfectly she could visualize them all: The six who had never been equalled! And although she and Mary Ellen had not been great buddies at the time, she remembered it that way because she needed to.

A few yards away, on the same sidewalk, Peter Rayman said impatiently, "Coming?" It was not particularly cold out, and there was no wind, but he was exhausted. Light and tiny as Hope was, when a guy had to lift her bodily into the air 7,000 times in a row in order to learn a new routine, he got a little tired. Okay, okay, so it wasn't 7,000 times, he thought. So there's nobody in the whole high school who weighs less than Hope. Still, I'm tired. I admit it.

But Hope Chang did not walk over to the car with him. "Peter," she said softly, "I think maybe I'll get a ride home with Olivia's mother. I need to talk a few things over with Olivia, and this is a good time. I'll see you tomorrow, okay?"

She smiled. There was a beauty to her face that never failed to strike Peter. Perhaps it was the color of her complexion, or the creamy smoothness of her skin; perhaps it was the slow way a smile spread on Hope's face. But he loved it. Now he chided himself for ever having abandoned

Hope to run after Diana. Especially when Diana turned out to be such a creep.

A hard-to-get-rid-of creep.

Beautiful, yes. It was Peter's first experience with beauty disguising a nasty personality. He couldn't get over the feeling that anybody beautiful ought to be good, also. He kept forgiving Diana and being friends with her anyway.

Maybe he and Hope should talk about that.

Yes. One of these days, Peter would take Hope out just to have a heavy talk. He'd even draw up an agenda. That would amuse Hope. They'd work their way through all their problems and come out giggling.

It did not occur to Peter to ask Hope what it was she needed to go over with Olivia. He dealt with his own feelings and forgot to think about Hope's. He didn't know that Hope was far more tired than Peter would ever be. Peter was physically tired, and that you could sleep off, but Hope was emotionally tired, and that was ever so much harder to get rid of.

Perhaps it's just the late winter, Hope Chang thought. I have cabin fever. I need some good, strong sunshine and a change of pace.

She did not say much of a good-bye to Peter. Holding her schoolbooks against her chest, she simply smiled again and swerved lightly to walk down the sidewalk to Olivia. The sidewalk was filled with puddles, and she stepped around them. She had new boots. Actually she had *two* new pairs of boots, and she loved them both and was alternating days wearing them. These were a soft dark leather, supple and rich, ankle-high, and not practical for a north country winter, but oh, so stylish! She loved how her slim ankles came up out of the angled boot top. Today she wore bright crimson tights, a slate gray skirt, a crimson shirt, and a black vest. She was so small it was hard to find clothing sophisticated enough in her size, but this outfit was perfect.

Peter hadn't noticed it.

He had not noticed yesterday, either, when she wore new pants, bought on sale at Marnie's, tight at the ankle and loose everywhere else, a nubby, costly fabric that looked like silk and felt like it, too. She'd had on an oversize blouse in vivid splash colors belted loosely down on her hips with a sash she tied three times around her body and let dangle down her thigh.

I want a boyfriend who notices me, she thought discontentedly. What's the point of dating a boy who doesn't really see me? Peter knows me only as a weight: a symmetrical thing to hoist once or twice during a routine. I'm so tired of that! I want him to —

But *did* she want him? At all?

Hope was beginning to wonder.

The parents she had considered rebelling against weren't crazy about Peter. Were they right? Was Peter worthy of their somewhat low opinion, or of her original high opinion?

Or was it just winter?

Up here in the north country, you could blame a lot of bad things on the tail end of winter. Everybody got stir crazy and cranky. She could not get rid of a perfectly fine boyfriend just because it was cold and raining.

"Liv, may I have a ride home with you?" she said to the captain of the squad.

Olivia was startled. "You're not going with Peter?"

"No. I wanted to talk to you."

More problems, Olivia thought, sagging even more. But she remembered her position as captain and said, "Sure. How can I help?"

Hope was smiling. "Oh, Olivia, what a sweetheart you are. No, it's not my problem. I don't think it is, anyway. It's Tara. I wish she weren't friends with Diana. What are we going to do? Diana wasn't sitting in the bleachers today at practice the way she usually is, but I felt as if she were! Didn't you? Couldn't you just *feel* Diana plotting ten feet above us? Looking down and scheming?"

Olivia dropped all her things in the rain to give Hope a hug. "You don't know how glad I am to hear you say that! I thought I was being sick and mean because of the way I feel about Tara and Diana."

"You're not." Hope shook her head. "My theory is that Diana is telling Tara that — "

But what Hope's theory was, Olivia never learned. It was not Olivia's mother's car that appeared out of the rain to drive her home.

It was Pres Tilford's Porsche.

Olivia felt as if she'd been tossed into a time warp.

For it was Mary Ellen Kirkwood sitting in the

passenger seat, laughing, her silky blonde hair tossed back and slipping forward again. her perfect hands gesturing in the air as she told Pres something. The beautiful, sleek car slid through the rain, and the occupants in it wore neither coat nor scarf. Insulated from the weather, they looked so handsome and so beautiful that they seemed also insulated from the world, and from everyday, boring problems.

Oh, to be Mary Ellen, or Pres — for whom all things seemed so easy! Olivia thought.

But the spell was quickly broken.

Pres saw her, grinned, and yelled through the windshield. She couldn't hear the words, of course, but she could see his lips moving, as he leaned on the horn, blew an unknown Morse code pattern, flashed his bright lights, and rolled down his window just as he pulled up next to Olivia and Hope.

"Hi!" he said, with tremendous enthusiasm. "Look who's here! Can you believe this, Olivia? Mary Ellen's come home for good! Isn't that the best news you've had in months?"

Olivia had to laugh. There were many months when it would have been the *worst* news. Mary Ellen coming back? Mary Ellen, the perfect? Mary Ellen, the captain to surpass all captains — coming back to show up Olivia. Last October, that had nearly occurred.

But tonight Pres was right. It *was* the best thing.

How wonderful Mary Ellen looked! So much more sophisticated than when she left; so much more . . . well, *urban*. She had a city look, not a Tarenton look. It wasn't just the clothes. It was also the set of her jaw, the tilt of her head. She looked much older. Nice-older — not dreary-older.

"Oh, Melon!" she cried, using the silly nickname as a term of endearment. "Oh, Melon, I'm so glad to see you!"

And she was. Immensely glad. She ran around the car, and Mary Ellen opened the car door and hopped out, wearing only a thin shirt and a long-ish skirt against the winter — and they hugged. Rain that lay softly on Olivia's coat wet Mary Ellen's shirt, but Mary Ellen was so happy at the welcome she didn't care. None of her New York roommates had ever greeted her like that. They were always afraid she was going to get the modeling job instead of them, and evening greetings were reserved, suspicious. And to think I thought the cheerleading squad could get hostile! Mary Ellen thought, laughing. She hugged Olivia a second time, more fiercely.

It was good to be home.

Coming home didn't have to mean failure and humiliation. Olivia was not demanding to know why Mary Ellen wasn't out there being a cover girl. Olivia was just glad to see her.

Mary Ellen found herself crying, and Olivia found herself wiping away those tears with her own scarf. They giggled. "You'll freeze to death, you jerk," Olivia said. "Where's your coat?"

"Who are you, my mother?" Mary Ellen demanded, laughing. But she did get back into the warmth of the car. Pres smiled at her. It was a very intense smile, not his wide, silly, adolescent grin. Mary Ellen did not shiver from the cold. She shivered from the intensity of that smile. Almost forgetting Olivia, not even seeing Hope, Mary Ellen was transfixed by that smile.

"We have to get together!" Olivia cried. "How about tomorrow night?"

"Great idea," Pres said, pulling his eyes away from Mary Ellen. "Want to come over to my house? Mary Ellen will be there. We have a lot to catch up on. Why don't you come around suppertime, Livvy, and we'll have lasagna. I'm in a lasagna mood. Are you, Melon?"

"Always," Mary Ellen said.

And then Pres noticed Hope, standing quietly on the sidewalk, glad the reunion made them all so happy, but feeling completely left out. How wistful she looked! "You come, too, Hope," he said quickly.

"Now, Pres," she said. "I wasn't part of the old gang. Thanks for asking me, though."

"I mean it," Pres protested. "I want you to come."

"Great," Olivia said. "Hope and I will come together. See you at six, then. Oh, Melon, I'm *so* glad you're home!"

She stepped back from the Porsche, and Pres moved slowly on and disappeared into the rain, taking Mary Ellen home to her family. Olivia, still so excited she *had* to hug, hugged Hope, who giggled again. "Why'd you make me come along?" said Hope. "I'm just not part of that crowd."

"You've missed a lot." Olivia could have danced home. The sight of Mary Ellen had raised her spirits. Hope, seeing this, did not mention Tara and Diana again.

Instead she thought, Peter wasn't invited. I'm going to a party without my boyfriend.

And she was curiously glad. It would be a relief to be separated from Peter.

CHAPTER

3

Hope Chang had been in the Tilford mansion before, at large parties. There was nothing the Tilfords enjoyed more than entertaining, and they did it splendidly. No matter what the gathering, that enormous house had the perfect room for it, and the perfect atmosphere. Tonight, on a cold and windy evening, they gathered in what Hope thought of as the English country library. Red leather on the heavy furniture, oil portraits on the darkly papered walls, and a great fire blazing in a fireplace of fieldstone.

But tonight there were no crowds of laughing strangers. Hope, who did not normally rise to the occasion at big parties, was going to have to contribute. It made her very nervous, and even the welcoming coziness of the library did nothing to soothe her.

Mr. and Mrs. Tilford, in contrast to other past

years, were in a wonderful mood when they dealt with their only son. It was no secret in Tarenton that the happiest moment of Mr. Tilford's life was when his son finally said, "Yes, Dad, I'm going to work at the family company after all."

How it showed! There was a closeness between parents and son that had never existed until now: a peace. It was, reflected Hope, much more like the Chang family than what Pres's family had been throughout his adolescence. The Changs rarely argued. Her parents were calm and ordered, and if Hope ever felt the terrible anxieties of being a teenager, she was expected to deal with her turmoil in an intellectual and unrebellious way.

Now and then she regretted the Chang upbringing. Tonight, though, seeing Pres with his parents, Hope was glad for him, and glad her own life had always been like that: close and affectionate.

Mary Ellen was wearing clothing that was much more sophisticated than she'd have had on a year ago. How beautiful she looked! Sitting on the wide stone hearth with the flames roaring behind her golden hair, her cheeks were red with the heat, and her eyes sparkled with the delight of being so near Pres.

She's floating, Hope thought. My goodness. That's what I call falling in love *fast*.

Or perhaps the love had always been there, lying in the wings, waiting for the moment when they could fly toward each other.

Mary Ellen and Pres could not take their eyes off one another. Pres inched toward Mary Ellen, adjusting his seat, changing his plan, angling his body. Pretty soon he'd be sitting right in the coals of the fire, thought Hope, wanting to giggle.

How lovely it would be if Hope felt that way about some boy. For a brief time, she had adored Peter. But Peter had faded — or possibly he'd never been that important, anyway. Maybe, thought Hope, I just liked the *idea* of Peter. Her parents had not thought very highly of him. Had Hope's affection for Peter been a tiny bit of rebellion against her ordered household?

Hope's mind drifted to Peter, and drifted away. For whatever reasons, they were no longer close, and for whatever reasons, she did not seem to care much. Longingly, Hope sighed. Watching Pres and Mary Ellen was like seeing a film at high speed: *This is love blossoming.*

We should all be so lucky, Hope thought.

"Hope, dear, will you have soda, or would you like something hot on a night like this?" said Mrs. Tilford, smiling.

Hope laughed. "With a fire like that, I think I need a soda with plenty of ice to cool me off."

"And you, Olivia, what will you have?" Mrs. Tilford went on.

Olivia's boyfriend was not there, either. David Duffy was a part-time reporter for the local paper and that night he had "something more interesting" to go to. Duffy didn't consider a Tilford party worth passing up an assignment for. Olivia didn't mind. She was having too much fun watching Pres and Mary Ellen. Other people's romances were so much easier than your own. All you saw were smiles and laughter — or perhaps later on, the fights and the throwing things — but you didn't get all emotional and twisted up over other people's love lives. Right now Olivia was utterly happy just seeing Melon.

Mary Ellen was tipping toward Pres like part of a cheerleading routine. Olivia was dying to tell her how sweetly funny they looked, but that would spoil it.

"So, Melon," Pres said, "are you going to marry me?"

Everybody laughed. Mr. Tilford, Mrs. Tilford, and Mary Ellen. Pres, Olivia, and Hope. It was as if they'd been waiting all evening for this comical punch line.

But Hope Chang thought, He means it.

She stared at Pres. Traditionally handsome, his dark-blond hair fractionally too long, his blue eyes bluer in the firelight, and his grin so intense!

Wow, Hope thought. Imagine getting a marriage proposal at our age.

But, then, Mary Ellen was not Hope's age. Mary Ellen was nineteen and her time in New York City had matured her even more than that. Hope felt very young sitting in that room. She felt like some neighbor kid let in for a treat, shortly to be sent to bed so the grown-ups could relax together.

A tall, frosted glass of Coke was set lightly in Hope's hand. She had forgotten about asking for a drink, and the glass startled her. Taking it in both hands — which really made her feel like a toddler! — she lifted her face to thank Mrs. Tilford.

But it was not Mrs. Tilford who had handed her the drink.

A rather short, slim boy, perhaps two or three years older than Hope, was smiling at her. The Tilford smile — she would know it anywhere. But absolutely straight, nearly black hair framing that same fair Tilford complexion. He was like a compact Pres with dark hair.

"Why, thank you," Hope managed. And then, biting her lips, she murmured, "But who are you? Is this going to be a soap opera episode? Are you an unknown son returning home?"

The moment the words left her lips, Hope was appalled. What if he *was*? Wouldn't it be horrible if he really *was* the black sheep son or something?

Why do I joke? she thought miserably. I'm terrible at it. Jokes always go wrong for me. I'm straight and boring and there's nothing I can do about it. I should be home practicing my violin or doing my chemistry and not play-acting that I'm sophisticated.

But the boy laughed. It was no Tilford laugh. It was very low and chuckly. "I'm Avery Tilford," he said, "Pres's cousin. My folks live in Maine and I haven't visited Tarenton since I was about ten, so you've never laid eyes on me."

Hope was relieved. Putting out her hand to shake his, she realized too late that her hand was now wet and icy from holding her Coke. But Avery took it anyway and then hung onto it.

"That's some chilly hand. Maybe we should sit by the fire, too, and warm you up."

"It's only from the drink. Really, I'm not cold."

"I was kidding," Avery said, still smiling.

"Oh." Now Hope truly felt young and stupid. Mrs. Tilford rescued them. "Hope, darling, Avery is in deep and serious trouble back home." She was laughing when she said it. "He has dropped out of college. One semester, and then he didn't feel like going back. His parents went a little mad."

"I can imagine," said Hope, whose parents would have done the same.

Hope was a small girl and accustomed to looking up at all her classmates and their parents, but it startled her to see that Avery, too, had to look up at Mrs. Tilford. Why, he's not more than two inches taller than me! thought Hope. She liked that. It made Avery seem more friendly — literally, more on her level.

"I wanted to travel in Europe for nine months," Avery explained. "Don't you think that would have been great, Hope?"

He did a little dance to show how great it would have been, and since he was still holding Hope's hand (by now pretty toasty), she found herself dancing with him. There was no music, but he established a beat with his sliding shoulder and jutting chin and Hope, half giggling, matched the rhythm and the movement and they danced in silent synchronization. Avery nodded his approval of her dancing and she matched the nod, and for a moment she thought he would kiss her, but he didn't.

"Anyway," Avery said, still dancing, "Mom and Dad said they were not going to finance a trip to anything but factory work if I intended to quit college. They said if I did assembly line labor, I'd find out firsthand the value of a college education."

Hope was laughing out loud. "But you're crafty, aren't you?" she teased. "You arranged to do your factory labor here at Tarenton Fabricators, and instead of a cheap rooming house, you're with your cousin in his mansion on Fable Point. Almost the same as a trip to Europe after all."

They were Pres's eyes: bluer than blue, and much more startling than Pres's because of the black hair. Avery tilted his head slightly, and then she could see that he was wearing contact lenses. So the blue was only partly his own.

"He's working a forty-hour week," Mrs. Tilford said. "He's on shifts, too, and in four weeks he starts working nights. Then, Hope, my dear, we're going to see a new interest in college. Old Avery here is going to believe in higher education after all."

"I don't have anything against higher education, Aunt Felicia," Avery protested. "In fact, I loved school. I did graduate fourth in a class of four hundred, you know. I just can't sit there anymore. I don't want to hear another professor, see another book, or do another assignment. I need a rest. My parents don't understand. They think — "

"Whatever they think," Mrs. Tilford said, "I'm on their side. Around here we have a house specialty in not going to college." Her eyes rested briefly on Pres. Pres's eyes were still fastened to Mary Ellen. Mary Ellen's were glued to Pres's. Hope thought Mrs. Tilford was going to say something about Pres, but an adult couple Hope did not know suddenly appeared, and there was a lot of touching of cheeks and cries of, "How *are* you!" as the adults moved to another room.

Hope said, "I know what you mean, Avery. I get tired of school every year about this time. There's something about the end of winter that ruins your enthusiasm for anything."

Avery looked into Hope's eyes. Maybe he was showing off in front of his dazzling cousin Pres, or maybe the heat from the fireplace had gone to his head. Very softly Avery said, "I don't think it's ruined my enthusiasm for *everything*."

Very meaningfully he let the silence lengthen. He jutted his jaw forward slightly, and then sideways, flirtatiously, and he began dancing again, very slowly, all alone.

Hope, who didn't flirt and rarely relaxed, danced in a mirror image of what he did.

They didn't touch.

Had she ever danced a slow dance without touching?

It was most odd. And, of course, the oddest thing was there was no music.

"I can't stand it," Olivia remarked. "Romance to the left of me. Romance to the right of me. And me all alone and unloved in the middle."

"It's your own fault," Pres said. "You could have dragged Duffy over here, you know, Olivia."

"There's nothing romantic about dragging somebody."

"Stop complaining and put some music on," Mary Ellen said.

Olivia pretended to sulk, but she went over to the impressive stereo system almost hidden by the ornate woodwork of the library. Going through the cassette titles she picked one that had her own favorite songs. If she had not had the security of David Duffy in her heart, she could never have stayed. It would have killed her to see four people falling in love, and to have been lonely among them. As it was, Olivia felt an enormous affection for the rest. She wanted all five teenagers in the room to find a "happily ever after": a time in which they would always feel this warm and good, and always be friends and lovers.

She danced slowly to herself, half watching Mary Ellen and Pres, who were intertwined, and Hope and Avery, who had not yet touched. She thought of David Duffy, and of spring, which must surely come soon.

She forgot Diana, and she forgot Tara, and she forgot all things that go wrong and that hurt.

CHAPTER

It was important to Tara Armstrong to stay cool and relaxed in front of other people. She liked to wear her red hair long and smooth; she liked to admire her lovely complexion when it was flawless (and stay home when it was not); she even preferred clothing that looked freshly ironed, as opposed to the wrinkled look that had been "in" for a while.

But underneath her smooth exterior, Tara was a jumble of contradictions.

And never more so than in the empty school corridor before the Thursday game.

It seemed to Tara she no sooner got her life perfected to match her looks, than something screwed it up again. She no sooner found a neat boy to date and felt good about him, than he vanished. She no sooner was given a car and got some freedom than something went wrong, like that horrible episode with Diana not too long before. And now, Tara no sooner got past those emotions, than a whole new set of difficulties appeared.

Tara had a unique definition of what made life smooth. It had to revolve around her. She had to have the attention. That was a smooth life.

This happened rarely.

Take tonight. Was anybody paying the least attention to her? Had anybody even bothered to say hello? Had anybody mentioned that she'd taken a big risk and cut two inches off her glorious red mane of hair? Had anybody said they really liked the new pants she'd bought the other day?

No.

Of course Pres and Mary Ellen sauntered around as if they still owned Tarenton High and, of course, everybody at Tarenton High ran up and assured them that yes, they *did* still own Tarenton High.

Olivia wasn't even pretending to be squad captain. She was just standing there clasping her hands, admiring the romance unfolding between Pres and Mary Ellen.

Jessica wasn't warming up or stretching. She was leaning tenderly against Patrick and also admiring the romance between Pres and Mary Ellen. How Tara resented it all! Here Patrick used to be in love with Mary Ellen. For years! His crush on Melon was so big that practically nothing else ever happened in Patrick's life except for the fact that Mary Ellen ignored him. And

Jessica had forgotten that ancient history, and so had Patrick, and they were just standing there, glad for two old friends.

Who was glad for Tara? she wanted to know.

And Sean, who was the cheerleader Tara would like to be dating — if she could just get their relationship off the ground again — was making remarks like, "I'd never get that serious over any dumb girl. Pres is not even acting like a person. He's totally gone on that blonde."

And then there was Hope.

You could count on Hope to be boring. Studying. Worrying about her violin or something. Now Hope was staring mindlessly at some cousin of Pres's. Some short guy who looked like yet another honor roll freak, with the Tilford money and the Tilford smile.

"Does anybody remember that we have a game in thirty minutes?" Tara asked acidly.

Nobody was listening to her.

Tara felt as if nobody had ever listened to her. No matter that she was eighteen and beautiful and interesting. She could talk all night and none of them would even bother to turn around.

They weren't even a squad.

They were just a collection of Mary Ellen fans.

Tara wanted to scream and make horrible faces and stick five fingers down her throat and pretend to gag.

She didn't, mainly because she *was* eighteen and didn't want to act like six. But she felt terribly angry.

Actually, she simply felt left out, but it hurt

too much to acknowledge that, so Tara pretended to be angry. She focused on how stupid they were instead of thinking how lonely she was.

She remembered one day the week before, after practice. Expecting to be given a ride home by somebody on the squad, Tara emerged after a shower and putting on fresh makeup to a gym that was dark and empty. The other five, who dressed quicker, had left without thinking of her. Nobody said, "Need a ride, Tara?" Nobody said, "Love those great earrings, Tara." Totally alone, Tara walked on silent rubber soles across the abandoned gym and saw, going past the exit, the young teacher with whom she had been so in love.

Nick, oh, Nick! Tara thought, and she yearned to race after him, fling herself on him, accept his love after all. For Nick Stewart had not chosen to end things; she had forced it upon him, to save his career. Dating a student would finish him.

But he walked swiftly on, and she managed to stay quiet in the dark, and now when she wept, in the cold silence of the gym, she was truly alone. And then . . . Diana was there. Full of comfort. Full of praise. Quick to compliment. Had the squad been good to Tara? No. Not once. She wasn't being loyal to the squad even to *talk* to Diana, whom they all detested . . . but it wasn't loyal of the squad to forget Tara, either.

So she accepted comfort from Diana, and she accepted a little advice, too, and now Diana was appearing at games and sitting behind her, as if they were buddies. Tara didn't know what to do about it.

It was all wrong, but she needed friendship too much to discard even Diana. And it all combined to make her angry and jealous and a little desperate.

Now, stepping back from the group of current and former cheerleaders, Tara pretended to be getting a drink of water from the fountain in the hall. A few fans buying tickets looked her way in surprise: Usually by now the cheerleaders were inside doing the pregame warm-ups. A few people even checked their watches to see if they were earlier than they'd thought.

You're not early, Tara thought. It's just that our esteemed, so-called captain is too busy gushing over somebody else's love life to remember her duties to the cheerleading squad.

If *I* was captain, it would be different!

For Patrick Henley, it was quite a thing to see his best friend with Mary Ellen. Somewhat to his surprise, he had no feeling left for Mary Ellen except mild affection. What a relief to know that all the agony and the ecstasy of his puppy love was gone, as if it had never been. How childish it seemed now! Those terrible years of yearning for her, driving after her, lying in wait for her, staring at her from afar, buying tiny gifts for her and then being afraid to give them.

And Pres! Patrick and Pres had had no use for each other for years. Then a closeness so strong developed between them that they were able to go into business together, defying Pres's parents together, and becoming adults together.

And now, unless Patrick was very much mistaken, Pres was feeling for Mary Ellen a much more adult emotion than either boy had ever felt before. Pres was standing with this girl the way you stood with someone you wanted to spend a lifetime with. This was not high school — even though they were standing outside the high school locker room.

Patrick's arms closed a little tighter around Jessica. He had dated her for quite a while now, and he knew that Jessica was the girl he wanted to live with forever. Jessica knew how he felt. She just wasn't there yet.

Yet.

A very important word. Patrick thought, Jessica will see how right it is for Mary Ellen and Pres, and how happy they are and how ready they are. And Jessica will want that, too. I'll get what I want from Jessica just by being a bystander watching Pres and Mary Ellen. Pretty painless, huh?

Patrick laughed silently, knowing Jessica could feel his laugh through his hug. Jessica graduates in June, he thought. I've always wanted a June wedding. I may be only nineteen, but I'm a self-supporting, successful businessman and I'm ready.

He squeezed Jessica gently, feeling the rough letter on her soft cheerleading sweater. It made him so happy to see his two old friends with starry eyes. Patrick knew the girl leaning against him had eyes just as starry.

Diana Tucker felt no starriness, no loneliness,

and no affection. She was simply jealous. She was swamped with jealousy, drowning in it.

That disgusting spectacle of Mary Ellen, swaying back and forth against Pres Tilford, as if they were being filmed! And all because they used to be cheerleaders, they could swagger around this dumb country school a whole year after they graduated and people would still pause to admire them, and let them have their way, and let them play at being king and queen.

Diana walked right into the locker room hall. There was a huge mirror just inside the locker room, and standing in the hall door she could see her reflection. Quite a resemblance to Mary Ellen. Same long, blonde hair; same figure; same wide smile; same clear complexion.

So why did Mary Ellen Kirkwood have it all? Why was Diana on the fringes still? Diana hated the fringes. She had moved to this dump of a town from California, and it seemed to her that that alone should have guaranteed her a space on the cheerleading squad, if not in the Miss America contest. Tarenton should consider itself darned lucky she was here at all, instead of ignoring her at every turn.

Diana wanted the squad.

She wanted the attention it conferred, and the friendships it passed out, and the pretty uniforms that graced its members. She had tried every means she knew of to get on the squad, and none had worked. Now, smiling to herself, she thought of another.

* * *

Jessica's thoughts were completely out of step with everybody else's. The only thing she could think was, They're crazy. They've got their whole lives in front of them to be serious in. What do they want to be serious now for? You couldn't *pay* me to get attached like that.

They're nineteen.

I might get married when I'm twenty-five. At the absolute earliest. I think twenty-eight would be better.

Did Mary Ellen know what everybody was thinking? Did she think it, too? Or was Mary Ellen just taking a breather from modeling — just acting in front of the old hometown? Had Mary Ellen's thoughts leaped from one evening with Pres to planning a whole lifetime with him?

Their eyes locked in such an intense way! You couldn't believe they were wondering who would win the basketball game. You knew they had to be planning their future children's names, or something like that.

Okay, Jessica thought. I do not want to ruin my senior year. And I'm very fond of Patrick. We'll still go out. Stay together for the proms and all. But I'm going to keep things on a much more casual level. I don't want Patrick to get any ideas watching those two. I'm certainly not going off the deep end just because Mary Ellen has.

Peter Rayman barely saw Mary Ellen and Pres. Even if he had glanced their way, he would have seen only a girl standing next to a boy. But he saw Hope, and he looked into Hope's eyes, and he knew exactly what he saw there.

A girl who had forgotten that he, Peter, existed.

Hope was standing at the angle where the hall to the cheerleaders' locker room intersected with the main corridor. She was about an inch inside the protruding wall. Approximately an inch outside the angle stood a kid Peter had never seen before. You could tell he was a Tilford by the smile and the arrogance.

But he was short, not athletic, and he was dark, not blond.

Hope was giggly, and swaying back and forth, shifting her weight from one foot to another and smiling at the kid.

She acted fascinated.

He, Peter, was taller, definitely more handsome, certainly had a better body. Peter was a fine athlete — not as broad or muscular as Sean, but still impressive in his own way. This kid looked like maybe on a good day he might turn a page in a book for exercise.

Sean Dubrow stood close to Peter. Sean's arms were folded and he was leaning back against the wall making snide remarks about love in general and Pres in particular. "He's a jerk," Sean observed.

"He's in love," Peter said, glancing briefly at Pres and immediately getting bored. Who cared about somebody else's love life? Unless that somebody else was Hope. Now that she was flirting with another boy, Peter was infinitely more aware of her.

Was she flirting?

Maybe she wanted Peter to rescue her. Maybe the guy was a nerd and a fool, and Hope needed Peter to come get her out of this.

Peter didn't make a move toward them.

There was something very tight about those two. They weren't touching and he was pretty sure they weren't going to touch. But all the same they were locked together. And he thought he knew all Hope's friends!

"So who's this guy with your girl?" Sean demanded.

"What's the matter with your attitude tonight?" Peter asked. "I don't know who he is. Nobody that counts."

Sean snorted. "You're as much of a jerk as Pres if you don't go over there and get her back. Women love that. They love to be told what to do."

Peter was dubious. It was not his experience that women liked to be ordered around. Hope was easygoing and she certainly obeyed her parents, but he had not observed any desire on Hope's part to take orders from him.

"Whatsa matter?" Sean said. "Peter, you gotta be aggressive. I think the guy's gonna ask her out. I can tell the way he's looking at her. Look how he's kind of turning his head sideways and staring down at his shoes all of a sudden. He's getting ready, Peter. He's trying to get geared up to ask for the first date. Look, look — now he's taking a big breath. See his chest expand?"

"His *little* chest," Peter pointed out.

41

The boys laughed rudely.

Nobody noticed Diana.

Cheerleaders could not wear watches or jewelry during a game. They knew the time from the large wall clock beside the full-length mirror between the locker rooms. Nobody saw Diana slip up, pry up the clear plastic lid with a quick flip of her nail file, turn the hands back fifteen minutes, and pop the lid back on the clock.

The cheerleaders were absorbed in themselves. The rest of the world, and their function in it, had vanished.

Avery Tilford thought, Okay, Hope, I'm going to ask you out. Say yes, say yes!

Patrick Henley thought, Okay Jessica, I want to be officially engaged. Say yes, Jessica, please say yes!

Tara Armstrong thought, I want to be captain of this squad. I want them to vote Olivia out and me in. Say yes — please say yes!

Jessica thought, I'm going to ask Patrick if we can be just friends for a while. Back off, Patrick, please don't be hurt. Please say yes.

CHAPTER 5

"*I am so disgusted with you!*" Ardith Engborg hissed. Her small frame was shuddering with wrath. She was angry enough to hit something, or someone, and the six cheerleaders, who all, including Hope, were taller than Ardith, trembled before her.

"I'm sorry," Olivia whispered through stiff lips.

"You're sorry," Ardith said acidly. "Well, well, well. She's sorry. And what good does that do, Miss Captain? Does being sorry change the fact that this cheerleading squad skipped its entire pregame routine? Does being sorry change the fact that when the basketball team ran out on the court, there was no squad lined up to announce them? No squad lined up to start the crowd cheers?"

"No," Olivia whispered. She could not look at anybody else. She was blinded with wretchedness.

43

She could feel her body twist, as if she could actually shrink away from her mistake.

"The six of you!" Ardith spat out. "Standing here! Lounging around! Not bothering to glance at the clock. Gossiping, or whatever it is you spend your precious time doing!"

Even Sean, who rarely worried about anything, felt nausea over what had happened. There they had been, just as their coach described, lounging around, gossiping — and all of a sudden the first three notes of "The Star-Spangled Banner" had begun on solo trumpet.

Impossible! the six had thought, leaping forward. They had always been out a good ten, if not fifteen minutes before the national anthem was played.

Olivia was supposed to have had the American flag out in center court. Tara was supposed to have been holding the state flag. It was Sean and Peter's job to hold the long, beribboned school banner.

The game couldn't have been starting!

The squad had burst through the door into the gym — to see a packed audience standing, hands on hearts, listening to the band play the national anthem. Both teams were on the court, ready to go. Warm-up was over.

And the captain of Garrison High's cheerleading squad had stood calmly in the center of the gymnasium, holding the long, heavy staff of the American flag high. She was beautiful, tall, and graceful. Staring straight ahead, she had given no sign that it was totally out of line for the visiting team to be doing this.

"I can't even discuss it," Ardith said. "I'm going to have cardiac arrest."

She really was hyperventilating. The rest of the squad was breathing right along with her, still totally humiliated two and a half hours later.

Half time.

The principal. The basketball coach. The two assistant coaches. All their parents. All their friends. All their friends' parents. All the alumni. "Uh, guys? You have some kind of problem here? You think maybe it's funny not to show up for our national anthem? You cheerleaders have something better to do, maybe?"

Apologies.

Cheeks scarlet with embarrassment.

Absolutely no idea how all six of them could have screwed up so royally.

Now in front of the locker rooms they were almost grateful for Ardith's chewing out. At least the crowd was leaving. Fewer people would be left to yell at them again when they finally emerged.

If we emerge, Hope thought. Ardith may commit a few homicides here.

"I thought I checked the clock, Mrs. Engborg," Olivia said miserably. "I thought I looked in and saw that we had plenty of time. I'm very, very sorry."

Ardith made a big deal of turning around and studying the large clock on the wall by the full-length mirror. "Funny," she said sarcastically. "It seems to be exactly on time."

It's my fault, too, Hope thought. I was really wrapped up in Avery. I never thought of glancing at the clock. I guess I just figured we'd automatically go out when we needed to be out.

Standing a few yards away, around the corner from the narrow locker room hallway, Pres and Mary Ellen winced at the horrible verbal beating the squad was taking.

"It's partly our fault," Mary Ellen murmured. "We were distracting them. We know better."

Pres put his arm around her waist. Actually his arm had never *left* her waist, but now he tightened it possessively, and led her away so they could talk without being overheard by Ardith.

"I think we have to admit at last that we just aren't Tarenton High cheerleaders anymore," Pres said. "For some reason I've had a terrible time facing that. Our year together was one of the most exciting of my life, and I guess I haven't wanted to surrender it. But it's time, Melon. You and I are moving on to other things."

Mary Ellen loved his arm around her, his face close to hers, and most of all the way every single sentence began with "You and I" or "we." To be a true team after this hard, hard year of loneliness! I guess that's what we all want out of life, Mary Ellen thought. A team of our own. Someone to belong to. Someone to root for.

She turned to look into his eyes again. It was

their lips that met, barely grazing, and yet the fierceness of it was enough that they had to pull away and catch their breath and force themselves to stay calm.

Wow, Mary Ellen thought.

With an effort she took up a new subject. "I was going to go sign up for classes at the junior college," she said, "but my mother pointed out it's midsemester. So I'm going to look for work tomorrow. Remember how I wanted to start work at the day-care center?"

Pres nodded. The whole concept was so unappealing to him he couldn't even address the subject. He was very grateful to be inheriting an enormous factory: How much more his style than diapers!

"Well, I called up two in existence. They're both delighted to find more help. And Pres, I can work the same hours you do! Seven A.M. to three P.M., because most parents are working at Tarenton Fabricators anyhow. Isn't that great?"

"Yes," Pres said happily. "You know, I never thought I'd be thrilled to start work at seven A.M., because if there's one thing I love, it's sleeping late. But now that I'm used to the schedule, I like it. There's so much of the day left when you've finished work."

Spontaneously they hugged each other and giggled, and even though they had been with each other only three days, they already knew how those free afternoons and evenings would be spent.

With each other.

Arms linked, hearts linked, they walked down halls they had once known so well as students, accepting without more talk that it was time to back off, and begin their own adult lives.

They forgot the terrible tongue-lashing the squad was taking, and talked only of themselves. There was so much to say! Mary Ellen felt as if there would never be enough time to cover all the topics she wanted to discuss with Pres. Pres felt there had never been company so responsive and so perfect as Mary Ellen. He could not imagine why he had not realized this years ago.

They planned their time. They would walk around the lake. They would go to Deer Park, an all year amusement park an hour's drive away. They would see every movie playing anywhere. They would learn how to make candy in Pres's kitchen and play tennis at the indoor courts and throw terrific parties.

"And after that, let's get married," Pres said.

Mary Ellen giggled. "I've told you and told you, Pres. I can't marry somebody who doesn't propose *right*."

"Oh," Pres said, pretending to jot this down. "Okay. Got it."

They both laughed, and squeezed each other.

The game was won by a mere three points.

Mr. and Mrs. Tilford surprised themselves by cheering as lustily as everybody else in Tarenton. They were utterly exhausted by the game they had not played. Saying hello to dozens of acquaintances, they drifted out by the locker rooms, thinking they would catch up to Pres there.

Avery, bored by all things athletic, dragged after them. Only Hope made the entire dull game worth sitting through. He sincerely hoped his aunt and uncle weren't going to make a habit of attending sports events. Even college lectures were better than spending his nights staring at a high school ball game.

Just as Ardith's voice reached a crescendo of rage, the Tilfords reached the hall to the locker room.

"Hmmmm," Avery said.

"Perhaps we should retire to the front foyer and pretend we didn't hear any of that," his aunt said. The three abandoned the hall and went out front. "Exciting game, though, wasn't it?" she said to Avery.

"No. Sports are dull. The best you can say for basketball is it happens quickly. Reasonable people don't spend their lives whacking balls of various sizes through nets, into holes, and across fields. The only games I can stand require thought. Trivial Pursuit or Scrabble or Scruples."

"Sssssshhhh," his uncle said. "We used to think that, too. We had no interest in this stuff, and I cringed every time Pres said he wanted us to come. But we sort of got enthralled by it. It's fun. And this is the most sports-oriented crowd you'll ever hope to meet."

"Speaking of Hope," Avery said.

They laughed. "Now she could be an excep-

49

tion," said his Aunt Felicia. "She comes from a very intellectual family. I know her mother slightly. Mrs. Chang donated a beautiful painting last year for the annual hospital auxiliary auction." Mrs. Tilford was very good at coaxing money or gifts from people. "I heard a concert once," she said, "in which Hope played the violin. Very talented, and an honor student as well."

"Hmmmm. Things are looking up," Avery said.

His uncle teased him. "Not very far up. You and Hope are too short."

They all grinned.

It was a good year in the Tilford family. There had been whole years in which they fought solidly. It was easy to lock horns with a boy as stubborn and difficult as Pres. But now life was smooth and they enjoyed each other's company.

Like roses in June, Felicia Tilford thought, glancing around for her beloved son. The thorns of Pres's hard adolescence seemed to have disappeared, and only the flowers and perfume remained to rejoice in.

In the locker room, Mrs. Engborg finally ran out of words to fling at her luckless cheerleaders. Nobody had arguments or defenses to give.

Then came her last words. Like gunshot they spattered over the six, to be heard clearly to anyone in the adjacent hall.

"Olivia, for whatever reasons, this squad has had morale problems on and off all year. I con-

50

sider it the captain's responsibility to deal properly with this sort of thing. And here you can't even get your squad to a game six yards away, let alone raise morale. I am giving you one more chance."

Nobody breathed.

"If things don't improve," said their coach, "I expect you to offer your resignation as captain and I will appoint a successor."

How they all ached for Olivia! Promising themselves to struggle harder for her sake, each of the other five wondered whether to speak up and defend Olivia. But what could they say? They could not imagine how this had happened. Even Tara was sick about it. Much as she yearned to be captain, she did not really want Olivia hurt in the process. She just wanted her out.

Stealing a glance at Olivia, Tara saw her captain look like stone: frozen in torment.

Ardith Engborg stalked out of sight.

Hope and Jessica sat down on a bench to recover. Peter wiped his forehead. Tara brushed her hair as if trying to beat it to death. "Wow," Sean said. "Glad that's over. Listen, Olivia, it isn't your fault. We *all* thought we had time."

Olivia said nothing.

David Duffy slid into the hall and saw the situation at a glance. He felt terrible for his girl friend. "Livvy," he murmured, arms around her, rubbing her shoulders to give her a little comfort and relief. But she didn't respond at all.

She was thinking that she should have offered her resignation right then, when Ardith mentioned it. I admit it, Olivia thought. I'm not the captain Mary Ellen was. I'm worthless.

Nothing like this happened when Mary Ellen was captain.

Nothing like this happened before in Tarenton High history.

It's me.

I'm a failure.

"You've been home three days," Gemma Kirkland said, "and I've barely laid eyes on you, Mary Ellen."

Her beautiful older sister laughed joyously. Gemma Kirkland recognized love when she heard it, and turned on the light to take another look at this sister in love.

"You don't have to do that!" Mary Ellen exclaimed. "You were almost asleep, Gemma. I didn't mean to wake you up. I thought I could creep in here and slide under the covers and you'd never know when I got home."

"I *wanted* to know when you got home," Gemma protested. "I want to hear every single thing about your evening. Details, Mary Ellen. You can't skip a thing. Here you were in New York for eons and your letters home were rotten. Six lines long. Three words per line."

"My letters weren't that bad," her sister said. "Anyway, I telephoned when I had something to say."

Gemma snorted. "Sure. Three whole minutes of talk because nobody could afford any more.

And now you're home and you don't stay home even five minutes at a stretch, and I *still* don't know one thing."

Mary Ellen slipped out of her clothes and shivered in the cold room.

"If you don't start telling me details about you and Pres," threatened her little sister, "I will sabotage your wardrobe."

They laughed.

All their lives they had shared this tiny one-closet room. Clothing was everywhere: stacked in boxes, stuffed in bureau drawers, hung from rods that poked behind the bedroom door, and from a portable rod meant for temporary use when ironing. They often referred to their bedroom as "the closet" and they didn't mean the size: They meant the visible clothing. The two beds almost disappeared under the clothes. And of course Mary Ellen had spent every possible cent on even more outfits while in New York. Negotiating a path through the little room was virtually impossible without the lights on and a sure foot.

Mary Ellen had gone through a stage of bitterness. She had hated the room and had regarded it as a symbol of all the things her parents couldn't give her.

But she had outgrown that.

She was loved. Her parents loved her, her sister loved her, and she loved them back. It made all the difference. The crowded little household no longer seemed like a punishment, but more of a nest to which she could safely return. And having worked in New York so very, very hard, without once being successful or earning much money, she was a lot more understanding of her parents' inability to get rich.

I've grown up, she thought suddenly. Every other time I told myself I was grown-up, it was because I had a birthday, or went to the prom, or became captain of the cheerleading squad. But now I am *really* grown-up. I know who I am and what I want and what I need and what I can give others. I am a decade older than the cocky little cheerleader who went to Manhattan to take it by storm.

"Well," she said to her sister, tucking her knees up under her chin and wrapping herself in her comforter, "Pres is certainly spending a lot of time with me."

"I noticed."

Mary Ellen grinned. "I think we both needed work, not school. We both had to flounder around. I had to try modeling and he had to try the moving business with Patrick. But now we've found ourselves. He's going to learn every aspect of his factory, and I'm going to work for a few years for a day-care center and then maybe open my own. And meanwhile — "

Mary Ellen paused.

Meanwhile. Meanwhile what?

The word was filled with Preston Tilford III. The room and Mary Ellen's thoughts were overwhelmed by thinking of him. He seemed to be right there, wrapped in the same comforter, leaning on her shoulder, grinning at her, making her feel special.

Mary Ellen blinked. I must not get carried away, she thought. "Pres keeps proposing to me," she said, sharing the joke with her little sister. She told Gemma about each proposal.

How cold it was in their bedroom. Her parents were really trying to save on fuel! She slid under the covers and tucked herself under the heavy blankets. Same old bed, same old town. It was pretty nice, really.

Without realizing it, she fell asleep.

Gemma got out of bed and turned off the light.

She was fourteen. Not the beauty nor the athlete her sister was, Gemma had never felt jealous of her sister, just a deep pride. Gemma was a happy person. She had never felt the need to excel, nor had the energy to accomplish excellence. Gemma had a gang of friends to laugh with, and she liked her life just fine.

So Pres Tilford was proposing to Mary Ellen hourly.

Gemma smiled into the thick, chilly dark.

Mary Ellen could think it was funny if she wanted. Gemma thought it was serious. Gemma thought Pres Tilford really would go out and find an apartment the next day and show it to Mary Ellen, to see if she would like to share it with him.

Gemma thought a June wedding would be perfect.

I'll be maid of honor, she thought. I look best in pink. If Mary Ellen wears an ivory gown, I'll wear pink with ivory lace, and my flowers will be baby's breath and white carnations and pink roses and soft, green ferns.

And Gemma, too, fell asleep, thinking, When he asks you for real, Mary Ellen, say yes!

CHAPTER

Gemma and Mary Ellen both woke to tapping on their windowpane. "What on earth?" moaned Mary Ellen. She fumbled for the clock-radio by her bed. "Six-thirty in the morning?" she said. Gemma rolled over and pulled the covers over her head. She didn't care *how* cute Pres and Mary Ellen were together; *nobody* was cute at 6:30 in the morning.

Clad in a long white flannel gown, printed with yellow flowers and tied with yellow ribbons (the best she could do in this cold house; her frothy gowns had to wait for summer), Mary Ellen staggered to the window.

Pres was plastered against it. His nose was flattened out and his lips were a caricature of a kiss. "I'm on my way to work!" he yelled through the storm window. "Had to say good morning first."

Mary Ellen pressed her nose opposite his and kissed him through the two layers of glass. Faces flat, their warm breath fogged everything until they were invisible to each other.

Mary Ellen grabbed a heavy robe, raced through the tiny house, and ran barefoot outside. "Come on in, dumbo. We've got ten whole minutes."

He took her hand and they sped back inside, panting. "True love," Mary Ellen said, pointing to her blue feet. "Getting frostbite all for you, Pres."

Pres kissed her without the glass between them. Much more satisfying. "Does this mean there's hope?" he said. "Are you going to accept me this time? Huh, huh, huh? Let's get married, okay? Can we, huh?"

She was too busy rubbing warmth back into her feet to reply.

They sat on the couch and snuggled. His ski jacket was slippery and icy against her, and she shivered happily.

He was comfortable in her house, but always aware of how very crowded and dark it was. The Kirkwoods needed another three or four rooms.

If I found a nice apartment, he thought, and we lived together, we'd have nice furniture. I could take care of her.

He had no more time, and headed for his Porsche. But Mary Ellen hardly noticed her own poverty. Time was she would not even have friends over after school, she hated her house so.

Now she scarcely saw it; her eyes were focused exclusively on Pres.

Her parents were getting up, too, as Pres drove off. Mrs. Kirkwood said, "Honey, I'd be happier if you didn't greet boys in your bathrobe."

But her father grinned. "She's more hidden in that than she is in her bikini."

"That's different," Mrs. Kirkwood said.

In the kitchen they buttered their toast and flipped their eggs over easy.

Gemma said, "Pres keeps proposing to Melon."

"Proposing what?" Mr. Kirkwood asked.

"Marriage," Gemma said, crunching Cheerios.

Mr. and Mrs. Kirkwood choked on their toast. The girls leaped up to whack their backs. After a crazy interval of slaps, chokes, snorts, and giggles, they were back to normal. "Forget it," Mr. Kirkwood said. "You're nineteen. Over my dead body, marriage. And Pres is immature."

"Daddy, Gemma's exaggerating," Mary Ellen said. "Pres is just playing games. He doesn't mean a thing."

"Told you he was immature," her father pointed out.

An hour later, six cheerleaders in their first class of the day were taking a real beating. Everybody who had been at the game to witness the Garrison flag-holding, and everybody who had not, made a point of saying something about the missing cheerleaders.

"Our own squad has to send out for reinforcements, huh?" one of the kids said.

"Guest cheerleaders," another said. "I like it. New idea. For when your current squad isn't up to standard."

In math there was a quiz first thing. Tara, too upset to study last night when she got home from the game, failed miserably.

The girl next to her glanced at Tara's pitiful score. "Not surprising," she said loudly. "An empty-headed rah-rah who can't even tell time. What can you expect?"

"Maybe it's 'cause her watch has a dial," one of the boys said. "That kind of clock is tough hauling, you know. You want I should lend you my digital clock next game, Tara? Little easier to read for the slow-to-catch-on."

"The slow-to-notice-basketball-teams-running-by," someone added.

"The slow-to-notice-the-national-anthem-being-played."

Tara grit her teeth. Bad enough that earlier in the year she had fallen in love with a new teacher and had to get through that. Bad enough her grades weren't great and she had to stay at school and work in spite of that agony. But to be on a squad that screwed up? Horrible.

Diana was in her math class.

Diana got an 88 on the quiz without trying. For a moment Diana admired her grade and thought how well, how impressively well, she could do if she ever felt like trying. She didn't feel like it, but it was good to know how smart she really was. "We don't really need guest cheerleaders," Diana said gently. "We need a whole new squad."

"Now there's a thought," another girl said. "Maybe we should start a petition."

Tara wanted to throw her math book at all of them, but the teacher said he would like to try teaching a little math, if it wasn't interfering too much with their plans.

Tara didn't listen. She had a problem of her own and didn't care about the one on the blackboard. Her eyes fell on Diana, copying the problem into her notebook. How lovely Diana was. Really remarkably like Mary Ellen. If Diana got on the squad, and later became captain, everybody would think the clock had turned back and the fabulous legendary old squad was —

The clock had turned back.

Tara sucked in her breath. They put their watches in their lockers when they dressed in uniform. They used the wall clock in the hall. Simple enough to hop on the bench there, pry up the lid, swing the hands back. Simple enough to correct that change as soon as the squad raced out of the locker rooms.

Diana frowned slightly, concentrating on the math problem.

Would Diana do that? Tara thought.

Of course she would. In a heartbeat.

Why, Diana, I could strangle you with your own yellow hair! You're sick, disgusting, horrible . . . but clever. Tara had to admit she was clever.

But I can't prove it, Tara thought.

She could tell the squad her suspicion, and the hatred for Diana would come to a boil and Olivia would be exonerated.

Or she could say nothing. Let Olivia feel wretched and be treated with contempt by their coach.

What's the matter with me? Tara thought. Why can't I be kind?

And then she said to herself rather firmly, Kindness has nothing to do with it. I have no facts to go on. I can't run around gossiping and guessing. Things will have to work out however they will, without my assistance.

A petition.

She doubted anybody would go that far. But Diana would tell Mrs. Engborg about the suggestion, and Mrs. Engborg would say something scathing to Olivia, and would Olivia be so crushed she'd quit?

The goal of being captain had never seemed so close.

And never had Tara been so unsure if she really wanted it under those circumstances.

Hope took less teasing than the rest. She was so earnest and serious and dedicated that nobody ever considered blaming her. Mostly they felt sorry for Hope because she'd been part of it.

Hope and Peter shared two classes. During the long morning they exchanged many looks. "I feel like the biggest fool ever to pass through Tarenton High," Peter muttered.

"A great way to be immortalized," Hope agreed.

Peter half wished Hope would cry. He would take her in his arms and comfort her, and that would bring them back where they had been six months ago: in love, and thrilled with each other. He just didn't feel very emotional now. He didn't much care. He half wished there was somebody else, and half wished he was still crazy in love with Hope.

All halves.

Not enough emotion to push forward and stake a claim, and that in itself was depressing. Just made the day worse.

It was during their second class together that the history teacher was buzzed on the intercom. "Yes?" he said, hating the interruption.

"Hope Chang to the office, please," said a loud, nasal secretarial voice.

Hope panicked. Somebody was hurt. Or dead. Or the house had burned down. Hand at her throat, Hope jumped to her feet. It didn't cross her mind that it could be her grades, or cheerleading, or student council. She thought only of her family, and what dreadful news the principal might have for her. She didn't say a word, but ran out of the classroom, thinking, I have to be strong. Whatever it is, my family will need me.

Peter watched. I'm still her boyfriend. If there's something really wrong — and from the way she reacted, she was expecting something — I should go after her. Be there with her.

But for all he knew, the secretary just wanted to correct an address label on some mailing.

So Peter didn't move, class went on, and Hope was on her own.

"And that's all I can afford," Pres Tilford said into the phone.

The real estate agent explained that apartments in Tarenton were hard to come by. It just wasn't a renters' town. He couldn't just find a perfect apartment by snapping his fingers. He didn't know if —

"This is important," Pres said. "It has to be nice. Great neighborhood. Spacious and sunny and clean. Big closets," he added, thinking of Mary Ellen's room. His first present to her would be her own walk-in closet. Room for all the dresses she had now and all he'd get her later. "And an enclosed garage for my Porsche," he said, "that I can lock. Very, very important."

The agent said there wasn't anything available at this moment.

Pres said the agent should get to work, then, and *find* something.

The agent said he really was very busy and would get to it when he could.

Pres started to get rude, crude, and socially unacceptable, but remembered in time he was trying to impress Mary Ellen with how adult he was, so he said very politely, "Could you try, sir?"

"Well . . ." the agent said.

"Thank you," Pres said humbly.

* * *

"Fine," the director of Little Folks Day-care and After School Program said. "You may start Monday, Miss Kirkwood. We'll be so glad to have you with us!"

Start Monday, Mary Ellen thought.

How final that sounded. How scary.

There it was: her career, her life. Starting Monday. Real work. Eight hours a day, with a paycheck and a pension plan.

She could hardly grasp it. New York at its most scary and modeling at its most unsuccessful had never shaken her so completely.

That was all temporary, she thought. I guess I knew that all along. But this isn't kidding around. I'm talking about *for good.*

She had a moment of genuine fear, thinking, Life wasn't going to work out like this for me! I was going to have so much else! Spread my wings. Travel. Live in the city.

But for travel and spreading wings, you needed money. A lesson she had learned so painfully during childhood, and learned all over again every night in Manhattan.

"Fine," Mary Ellen said to the director. "I'll start Monday."

How short a vacation. Less than a week of flirting with Pres, of flirting with the whole high school, almost, and then back to work.

She didn't want her life to be grindingly hard, the way it was for her parents. She didn't want to eke out a grim living, skipping all the pretty things she yearned for. She wanted fun and laughter and good company.

And Pres Tilford.

Hope was panting when she reached the office. She made herself slow to a walk. Her rib cage hurt, but she composed her face, smoothed back her well-cut black hair, and walked sedately into the office.

The secretary glanced up and yawned.

Yawned? There could have been a car accident, Hope thought in a rage, and she's yawning.

"Phone call for you," the secretary said, yawning again. "Pick up line three. It's your Uncle Avery."

Hope's hand, half closed on the phone that sat on the wide counter, stayed suspended. "My Uncle Avery?" she repeated.

The secretary nodded again and yawned again. "My goodness," she said, "excuse me. We rented wonderful movies last night and I watched one of them twice. *The Blues Brothers.* Have you seen that? It's got my favorite line in it. The part where he says — "

"Yes," Hope said, "I've seen the movie." She took the phone, poked the button for line three, and said, "Hello?"

"Hello, Miss Chang, this is your Uncle Avery calling."

Avery Tilford. Hope turned her back to the secretary to hide the laughing expression rising to her face. "Yes, Uncle Avery?" she said, picturing him so easily. That dark hair and those Tilford eyes. He had to be laughing, too. She pictured him laughing. "Is something wrong?" she said. "Has there been an accident?"

"Your Uncle Avery has accidentally fallen in love," said Avery Tilford.

Behind her the secretary was quoting from *The Blues Brothers.* "It's a hundred and six miles to Chicago. We've got a full tank of gas, a half pack of cigarettes, it's dark out. . . ."

Hope choked on her giggles. "Sounds serious, Uncle Avery."

"It is. Much too serious to be resolved at any dull athletic event such as a basketball game. The only cure is going to be dinner for two, far removed from high school gymnasiums."

"Well, it's Friday night. And there's no game scheduled. So I could probably visit you in the hospital."

"And we're wearing sunglasses!" finished the secretary, yawning yet again.

"Actually I have the use of Uncle Preston's car. I'll pick you up."

"Should I bring the patient flowers?" Hope asked. "Or a good book?"

She could tell how tickled Avery was by the success of this crazy phone call. She was carrying it off as if they'd rehearsed it, and the secretary, done yawning, was now all worried about the patient who needed flowers. Avery said, "I'll bring the flowers. You bring the book. I like thrillers. Something for me to read during your next game when I'm bored out of my mind."

"How can you be bored when I'm cheering?"

67

demanded Hope, forgetting her role as Uncle Avery's niece.

"I want your personality, not your uniform."

"It's a complete set," Hope told him. "You don't get one without the other."

"Oh. I guess when you're hit as hard as I am, you take these minor difficulties in your stride."

Hope said, "You have to meet my parents first. They're very strict."

The secretary blinked. "Your uncle hasn't met your parents?"

"We're not a close family," Hope said sadly. She hung up on a laughing Avery Tilford and thanked the secretary for reminding her what a great movie *The Blues Brothers* was. "Maybe we'll rent that ourselves this weekend," Hope said. "We have to cheer up my uncle somehow."

"And that will bring the family together, too," said the secretary, who was happy about the whole thing.

But not as happy as Hope Chang.

CHAPTER

7

"**O**h, Patrick!" Jessica pushed her thick brown hair out of her eyes and sighed so heavily it almost brought her to tears. "I've never been so glad to see you. It's been such a terrible day. I feel as if the entire high school came out and whipped me." Jessica had little experience with being a fool. To be laughed at by several hundred kids! Ugh. She simply hated feeling stupid. "Tomorrow we have another big game," she told him, "but at least it's away. The other squad does the pregame show, and holds the flags and all that."

Normally Patrick worked till quite late in the afternoon, but today he'd found half an hour. He taped a note to Jessica's locker that he would pick her up after school and take her home. Leaving the van at the job, he just hoped the two new helpers could handle the rest of the unpacking on their own. They weren't too swift and he preferred to monitor their every move. But how far wrong could they go unpacking crates of lamps?

How lovely Jessica was.

And how annoying that he had only half an hour to give her — a full hour if he dared trust those two guys that long. He had jobs lined up continuously. He wouldn't see his girl friend again until Sunday. No way could he drive a van full of furniture across the entire state and get back in time for her game tomorrow.

If we lived together . . . he thought.

He played with the idea. "You've never been so glad to see me?" he repeated, staring at the high school senior he adored so much.

"Never." She pushed the seat belt away and slid over right next to him. Burrowing up against his shoulder, Jessica wrapped half his heavy jacket around herself for comfort and warmth. Patrick held her hard. He listened to her tales of woe: the cheerleading squad, Olivia, and the teasing. He felt infinitely older than Jessica.

She graduates in June, he thought. That's not so far away. It's March now. Slowly, slowly, the north country will turn warm. We'll go down to Pres's house and sail, and swim, and water-ski on the lake.

But he didn't want to do things with her in public like that. Parties and games. He wanted to spend time with her in private. Just the two of them.

He tried to imagine marriage.

It was foggy. Difficult to see himself there. But

he was sure he wanted it, sure he and Jessica could pull it off.

Patrick hated the thought of Jessica's college plans. The nearest college she had applied to was at least 500 miles from home. Whenever he considered that move, he felt angry and abandoned.

What was wrong with going to college right around here? Didn't she have any loyalty to him? Didn't she realize he needed her? And for that matter, didn't she realize *she* needed *him*?

It wasn't as if she'd find somebody better than Patrick Henley at her dumb old Eastern establishment colleges. Nineteen, and his two businesses provided a larger income than most men ten years his senior could earn. A thriving trash business. A growing moving business with more customers than he could handle, because word of mouth was the best advertising, and Patrick's work was excellent and courteous and on time. Patrick earned more in one year than his father did.

Why wasn't Jessica excited over that?

Why did she just shrug when he pointed out to her how well the two of them could live?

Once there had been a hangup over her dad's death. Mr. Bennett had died when Jessica was small, and for years she held back from attachments to other people. Fear that death would separate her again kept her from risking love. But thanks to Patrick, who had coaxed and persuaded, she was past that.

Now she had a new excuse for not getting engaged. She needed college, she said. She needed a career and lots of freedom. She was not ready to settle down, she said. She needed space, she said.

Talk about garbage, Patrick Henley thought. You don't find anything in my trash barrels more rubbishy than that talk.

She wants college — she can have it here.

She wants a career — it can be in Tarenton.

She wants space — I'll build her a big house.

He ran his fingers through her hair. She had braided a little of it along the sides and pulled the slender braids into a tiny rat tail. He detested that style. Slowly his right hand, curved affectionately around her, worked the braids out.

"Patrick, don't," Jessica said. "I want it that way."

"But I don't." He finished pulling the hair free. With his fingers he combed it back into the rest of her hair. Sighing, he saw by his watch the half hour was almost up. It didn't feel as if he had had any time with her at all. Jessica felt the tilt of his wrist as he glanced at the watch, and she immediately slid away from him and snapped her seat belt into position. Helplessly, Patrick drove her home.

He considered Jessica's family life: a mother who cringed, and a stepfather who didn't care about her. Jessica ought to be thrilled at the prospect of getting out.

And she was, he thought sadly. Thrilled at going off to college. Not thrilled at the idea of marrying him.

In moments they reached her house. She undid

the seat belt and slid quickly over the upholstery, planting a swift — very swift — kiss on his cheek. She slid back, opened the door fast, and hopped out. He hadn't wanted a kiss on the cheek. He wanted to sit there fifteen minutes kissing good-bye, every kind of kiss they'd ever known, over and over.

"Thanks, Patrick," Jessica said. He always fell for her soft, throaty voice, and he fell again now. "I always feel better when you call for me," she told him. "Like getting bailed out of jail."

Patrick grinned. "School can't be that bad."

"Today it was. Well, I'll see you Sunday."

She seemed awfully cheerful about it. Patrick reached out to touch her, but she withdrew and he missed her. Twinkling her fingers at him in good-bye, she darted into her house.

Glad to go indoors, Patrick thought. Was it just the cold wind? Or was it me, reaching toward her?

For a time he simply sat in the car, willing Jessica to peer out the window and wave, or blow a kiss, or maybe even come back out and give him the hug and kiss he yearned for.

But she didn't.

He hurt all over.

Finally he drove back to work. He put his mind entirely on the job at hand.

Women, he thought. You can't live with 'em and you can't live without 'em.

Olivia, raw and torn, waited in the halls for the Friday rush to end. No cheerleading practice.

73

That was one good thing, at least. She didn't have to face her squad after this horrid, horrid day, for which she was fully responsible.

How could a day be so long?

How could so many people think it was a good idea to mention her stupid failure?

If Mrs. Engborg had scheduled practice, Olivia would have compared notes with the other five. She'd have found out that even Sean, to whom everything was a joke, had been hurt by the teasing. She would have found that Tara and Jessica were both coming apart at the seams, that Peter was tied in knots, and that only Hope had somehow been left out of the general roasting.

She would have felt much, much better, sharing the humiliation.

But there was no practice, and Olivia didn't realize the rest were getting picked on as much as she was. She felt as if she did not have a friend or an ally in the world. Even the thought of getting together with Duffy did nothing to perk her up.

Little forest animals supposedly hid by themselves to lick their wounds until they were whole again. Olivia sympathized. She would like to crawl home in the dark and hide in her room for a few years.

At least it was Friday.

Kids emptied out of school on Fridays like bullets out of a shotgun.

Trudging to the main entrance, Olivia prepared to face the kids on the late bus. But up drove

Mary Ellen. In the Porsche! Olivia was startled out of her misery. "Melon!" she shouted, racing across the sidewalk. "Are you sharing his car now? Oh, Melon, you were born for that car. You look perfect in it. It's your color."

They laughed at the idea of choosing a car to match your complexion and hair, but it was true. The red set off Mary Ellen's blonde hair and blue eyes like a great, gleaming frame. "Hop in," Mary Ellen said. "I have so much to tell you. I'll give you a ride home. You don't want to take the late bus, anyhow."

"No sane person ever wants to take the late bus," Olivia agreed. I do have a friend, she thought, circling the Porsche and getting in on the passenger side. I have an old friend — a good friend — who seeks me out. Oh, Mary Ellen, thank you for coming home! I needed you.

Mary Ellen drove on. Where Pres accelerated quickly and the motor roared and a patch of rubber was left on the road, Mary Ellen drove gently. It seemed like an entirely different car with her driving. A stable, calm, middle-aged car, compared to Pres's wild stallion of a car.

"I had to go job-hunting," Mary Ellen said. "At lunchtime Pres came over with a guy from the factory to give me his Porsche for the afternoon, and then he drove back to work with the other guy in his car. How many girls go on their first job interview in a red Porsche?" she said, grinning happily.

The girls joked, and the laughter tugged at

Olivia's unhappiness and lifted it away. Mary Ellen chattered about her new job, and Olivia told about the terrible teasing in school.

"Oh, I remember that stuff!" Mary Ellen said with a shudder. "Remember that time people thought I might be shoplifting?"

They both shivered. What a test of team solidarity *that* had been!

"Remember how I used to cringe when Patrick would follow me around town in that garbage truck? The first one he had?"

"I remember. It was so garbagey looking," Olivia agreed. "I mean, you could not pretend it was anything but a garbage truck! You could smell it for blocks around!"

They burst into gales of laughter and began to reminisce about last year. The good year, as Olivia thought of it.

Mary Ellen was so full of herself, so happy, so very blonde and blue-eyed and laughing, that Olivia was swept up into Mary Ellen's joy.

On Saturday morning, the real estate agent took Pres and Mary Ellen to the only apartment that could possibly fit Pres Tilford's description.

"Perfect," Pres said, grinning from ear to ear. "We'll take it." He put his arm around Mary Ellen and squeezed her tight.

Mary Ellen laughed and shook her head. "We?" she repeated. "Pres, I don't know what you're thinking, but *we* aren't doing anything here. I just happen to be along for the ride. *You're* signing the lease."

Pres nodded. "Right. But do you like the place?"

Like it? Mary Ellen had to laugh. How could anybody not like it? It *was* perfect.

Only six houses away from Pres's own mansion, it was the second floor of another Fable Point mansion's carriage house. Built a hundred years ago, when houses were solid with character, it even had a stone fireplace. The kitchen window, small and bright, looked over the lake. From the dining room table you faced west, and the sun would set beyond a grove of tall firs. The living room was long and low, with slanting ceilings. The bathroom was large, with space for a chest of drawers and a chair. The bedroom was small, but had two enormous closets. All the walls were white, the floor wooden, and the whole feeling was crisp and clean, like a new start in life.

It was, she thought, a honeymoon cottage.

It was waiting for two people in love, who would light candles on the table and laugh in the dark.

"So?" Pres said impatiently. "Do you? Like it?"

"Oh, yes," she said. She thought of her parents: They never had even a week of bright-light easy life. Perhaps they never would. But Pres, whose life had always been cheerful, would be more cheerful. He would simply move on to another happy position, facing another sunset with its gaudy colors and then its peaceful dark.

What do I want? Mary Ellen Kirkwood thought.

She walked slowly through the apartment,

touching the backs of the wooden kitchen chairs, running her fingers over the nubby country fabric of the sofa.

I want happiness. I want fun. I want company.

"Then we'll take it," Pres told the real estate agent. He followed Mary Ellen and caught her from behind and hugged her tightly.

We. What did he mean, *we*?

She tried to think of herself as a unit with Pres. A pair. A couple.

This isn't high school, she thought. This isn't a trip to McDonald's here and a dance there and a movie next. He's talking a *real* pair. Preston Tilford III and Mary Ellen Kirkwood.

"Wonder if this would make a good dance floor," Pres said, moving his feet on the gleaming wood. He danced a few steps, and began to tug her with him, and they circled the sofa and turned between the chairs and across the space to the table.

The agent smiled. "I'll just run down to my car and get the papers, then," he said, "and you two can plan your wedding day."

Mary Ellen bit her lip.

Pres grinned and swung her in a circle.

"Pres," she said, "just what do you have in mind here?"

"I told you. Marriage. Haven't I proposed a thousand times?"

"Yes, but you're joking. I know we're crazy about each other. I know this is more intense than anything we've felt before. But — " She shook

78

her head. The idea of herself married was hard to come to terms with.

"I am not joking," Pres said firmly. He let go of her and walked into the bathroom and pulled a pink Kleenex out of a box on the vanity shelf. He folded it over four times and twisted the bottom between his fingers and began ruffling and tearing the folds. Slowly it turned into a pink rose, the kind you made in first grade and took to your mother for Mother's Day.

He dropped to one knee in front of her and handed her the Kleenex rose. "Mary Ellen," he said in a deep, faked voice, "my dear, will you wed me? Will you be my own? Forever, and ever, and ever, and ever, and ever, and — "

Mary Ellen stopped him by kissing him firmly. "I don't marry broken records," she told him.

They laughed and danced like little kids around the room until the real estate agent came puffing back up the stairs.

Do I really love Pres? Mary Ellen thought. She watched Pres read through the lease papers, a frown on his forehead, and she saw the adult Tilford businessman there: a glimpse of the adult Pres would be. Was he adult yet? He was acting like a teenager with her.

Pres read through the papers. He could not sublet, he could not have dogs, he could not this, and he could not that.

Do I really love her? he thought. Or am I just playing games? Or is love a game and that's the way all people in love play?

He'd spent a jillion hours with Patrick Henley. Patrick loved the whole idea of marriage, and had been trying to convince Jessica to get serious for months now. Pres had thought the whole idea of marriage was pretty scary.

And yet now he could think of nothing he wanted more.

He had the job, the future, and the energy. He wanted to get started being an adult. It seemed to him he needed Mary Ellen. He needed somebody to do all this *for*.

This is crazy, Pres thought, suddenly terrified by the whole thing. He handed the papers back to the agent, and his signature seemed very large and very permanent on that dotted line.

"Lot of southern windows," he said to Mary Ellen, feeling uneasy with her. Wanting to talk of nothing in particular. Safe topics. Like weather and southern exposures.

"Easy to heat," she agreed.

"But a nice view," Pres said.

"Especially at supper," she said. "Watching a sunset. I love sunsets."

"I didn't know that," Pres said.

They stared at each other from a distance of several feet.

Pres opened a kitchen cabinet. It made it possible to look away from her. Inside, plates were stacked: bright plastic in primary colors, glasses with pineapples on them, and mugs with impressively ugly flowers.

"Ugh," they said together.

"At least we get to buy something of our own," Pres pointed out.

Something of our own.

The words hung in the room. It was very possible. They could feel a life together right there, in this space, in front of that cabinet. Their lives, bound up for good — the next day, even. It was a future ready for the taking. It would take only a minute and a new set of china.

Mary Ellen shivered slightly. She turned, trying to admire the view over the lake, but seeing nothing.

Half of her wanted to hug Pres forever.

The other half wanted to run, run for miles, run across the entire continent. Get away from a love that could save her — or engulf her.

CHAPTER

8

"You are somewhat early, Avery," Dr. Chang said. "You may sit with me in the living room, if you like, and we will wait for Hope."

Oh, wow, Avery thought. What do I talk to this guy about? He seems so stern and serious. "Yes, sir," Avery said, because he could not possibly have called Hope's father anything but sir. "That would be nice."

Nice? It would be a disaster. Already Avery was worried. Faintly he could hear a solo violin. "Is that a record?" he asked dubiously. But the stereo set was on either side of him, and the speakers were silent.

"It's Hope."

Avery was astonished. "That's Hope? It sounds like a concert."

"It is a concert. She's given a number of recitals. She's preparing for another one. We hope she will stay with music in college and afterward, but she isn't sure she wants to. She has many interests, you know."

"I don't know," Avery admitted. "I hardly know her at all. But it's pretty exciting, Dr. Chang. She's really good, isn't she?"

He nodded and said, smiling, "And what are you good at, Avery?"

Avery was very glad he had a few things to mention. He would not like to be in this overachieving household and have to admit he was a jerk who did nothing. "I was pretty good at high school," he said. "I got nearly straight A's and I was fantastic in physics. I loved physics. I wanted to be an engineer. Geology and petroleum. As a matter of fact, I went to Polytech on early admissions."

Now *that* was something to brag about. He just hoped a family that specialized in classical music would know just how impressive early admission at Polytech was.

But instead of congratulating him, Dr. Chang leaned back in his chair and frowned slightly. "Odd time of year to be out of class," he said.

How could they have gotten to this touchy subject so fast? Avery wished Hope would finish up her symphony, or whatever it was, very quickly. "Well, sir," he said, dreading Dr. Chang's response, "I was having a hard time. In high school I could get a ninety-eight in physics without half trying. But once I got to the university, everybody was that good. And . . . well . . . I. . . ."

He wanted to stop talking about it. He hated

admitting that he had just panicked. The competition was so stiff, the classes so hard. Avery finished first semester with all C's — and one D. Avery was shocked. In all his life he had never been average. How could he have worked so hard and ended up so ordinary? Maybe he wasn't good enough after all, he thought, back at college.

Maybe I should quit, he had thought next.

And he had.

Abandoned the dormitory. Gone back home. And his parents gave him so much static he couldn't even retreat there. He had to flee across the country to his cousins.

Avery hadn't really talked about this to anybody. He'd been yelled at for it, yes. All his relatives had gotten into *that* act!

Now, to his surprise, he found himself spilling out his troubles to Dr. Chang. Hope's father sat quietly and nodded, asked a few careful questions, and nodded again. There was something very restful about the man. Just sitting there, facing him, Avery found himself feeling more calm about the whole rotten failure. Avery did not feel judged. Dr. Chang was simply sorting out the situation.

"Panic is not unusual," Dr. Chang said after a while. "Those of us accustomed to excellence get scared. It was unwise to abandon ship like that, Avery, but you will get back on board next fall. You will be more mature for the time off and do better. Don't feel you have failed. You have just withdrawn temporarily."

Avery had planned everything he would say to Hope tonight. But instead it was Dr. Chang

he talked to. His worries about college, his feelings about being an assembly line worker at a
factory instead of returning for a second semester — all of it poured forth.

He forgot Hope.

He no longer heard the violin.

He fixed his eyes on the small, quiet man who
simply listened and nodded and listened again.

Gemma Kirkwood telephoned Olivia.

"You're home," she said happily when Olivia
answered. "I thought you might be out with
David Duffy."

"Oh, he has some meeting to cover. Honestly,
I can't stand these people who are starting their
careers when they're still students. I think they
should concentrate on school," Olivia said.

Gemma giggled. "You mean, you think he
should concentrate on you."

"Exactly."

They talked for several minutes. Olivia was
surprised to get a phone call from Mary Ellen's
sister. She hardly knew Gemma. Tarenton High
was a big school, and the grades didn't mix much.
Gemma had never made a habit of hanging out
at cheerleader practices last year, the way Diana,
say, made a habit of it this year. Olivia tried to
imagine what Gemma would call her about. All
this small talk must lead to something.

I bet they're having a surprise party! she
thought. For Pres and Mary Ellen. Ooooh, that'll
be fun!

"Tell me about Pres and Mary Ellen," Gemma

85

ordered, abandoning chatter for the important part. "I see them at our house and Mary Ellen talks to me a little, but I want to know what they're like with all of you guys. Are they really, really, really in love?"

Olivia was disgusted. "Is that all you want?" she asked irritably. "And here my hopes were up for a surprise party. I've always wanted to be part of a surprise party."

"I'll give one once I know what we're celebrating," Gemma promised. "But I'm not a hundred percent sure yet. Do you think they'll get married?"

"*Married?*" Olivia shrieked. "One of *us*? Somebody *my* age? Get *married*? What, are you out of your mind?"

"No. But Pres and Mary Ellen are out of theirs."

Both ends of the telephone line were silent while Gemma and Olivia contemplated this.

"Wow," Olivia said finally. "Marriage. A wedding. Now *that* would be a surprise."

"Of course," Dr. Chang said finally, "we must first handle the problem right here before we tackle your college problems."

Avery did not know what problem they had right there.

"We have kept Hope waiting for over an hour, Avery," said Dr. Chang, smiling. "And now it's quite late. I'm not sure she should go out with you after all."

"Daddy!" Hope cried.

Avery jumped. She was standing in the doorway, had probably been there a long time. Flustered, Avery stood up, wondering if Hope realized he had literally forgotten her.

"I'm joking," her father said mildly. "Of course you can go out. Bring her back by midnight, Avery. You and I will finish our discussion next time you come over."

Hope nearly hauled him out of the house. "I didn't think the two of you would ever stop talking," she said to him, exasperated.

"Why didn't you say something?" Avery said. "I came over to take you out, after all. Not to talk to your dad."

Hope slid into his car. "I don't have that kind of family, Avery."

"What kind don't you have? The kind where the boy comes for the girl?"

"No, no. The kind where the daughter interrupts the father. You and Daddy were having a close conversation, and I couldn't interrupt."

Avery stared at her. "You weren't kidding, then. You really do have a strict family."

Hope kissed her fingertips and then pressed them to his cheek. "And welcome to the fold, Uncle Avery," she said teasingly. "Your little niece here is glad to see you."

Avery found himself wondering, in such a strict family, just what Hope would expect from him. How he should behave. Whether a kiss by remote control was as far as he could go.

This, Avery Tilford thought, is going to be fun.

For Mary Ellen, that day and all that followed whipped by.

She was emotionally dizzy. Rushed by Pres, harried by work, she felt life had picked up speed. It was going so fast she could scarcely focus on the scenery. It seemed to her she barely hugged her mother good-bye in the morning than she was dropping, exhausted, into bed at midnight.

There were mornings with tiny children: sweet, darling kids and nasty, runny-nosed kids; mornings with food and diapers and alphabets and songs and playgrounds; mornings of laughter and tears and scraped knees and lullabies at naptime.

Afternoons Pres came for her. She hardly noticed what they did together and it hardly mattered. They drove for miles, through deep pine woods, around the scores of lakes in the area. They went skating, to the movies, out for doughnuts, and out for pizza. They went to friends' houses and they went off by themselves. They sat countless hours in his living room or hers, and talked and talked and talked.

I have never been in love before, she thought.

Nothing ever felt this strong. Nothing ever obsessed me like this. Anything else was a mild crush or an adolescent heart surge. This is incredible. This is truly knocking me over.

When the two of them were at Pres's, his parents were often there, too. Once Mary Ellen had been so awed by Mrs. Tilford, she could hardly string two sentences together in front of that elegant woman. She felt stupid and lower-class and ignorant just thinking about Felicia Tilford.

Now she and Mrs. Tilford could laugh together, talk together, and fix dinner the occasional nights when there was no household help — yet Mrs. Tilford seemed just like some pleasant woman who happened to be standing there. The rooms were filled with Pres. Everything else — even his family standing next to him — receded.

One night she and Pres were sitting on the couch. They were careful not to touch, because Mr. Tilford was sitting in the red leather chair opposite and Mrs. Tilford was doing embroidery in the small upright chair by the lamp. Mary Ellen wanted to touch Pres so much, but she couldn't do it in front of the Tilfords.

But of course! Mary Ellen thought, amazed that she had not realized it sooner. They were always around because they were chaperones. The senior Tilfords were worried.

Mary Ellen studied Pres's mother. Mrs. Tilford was using a French knot to make white wool on a flock of sheep. Pres's mother looked up, caught Mary Ellen's eye, and smiled.

She likes me, Mary Ellen thought. I never thought she would. I thought she would want somebody better for Pres.

In a slightly strangled voice Pres said, "Let's go for a drive, Melon."

"You've been for two drives today already,"

his father said lightly. "Why don't we all play Trivial Pursuit or something?"

Pres said dryly to his father, "Dad, right now I don't have a single trivial feeling."

They all laughed. "I know son. That's what worries your mother and me. This seems very, very serious all of a sudden."

The four of them braced slightly, each wondering if there was going to be an argument or some painful scene. Certainly there had been plenty of those when Pres was in junior and senior high.

But Pres didn't snap back. He didn't scream that it was none of their business, or that they were trying to ruin his life, or that they were interfering. "It is serious, Dad," he said slowly. "But it's not sudden. Mary Ellen and I have been in classes together since kindergarten, and we know each other pretty well."

"You must admit," his father said very carefully, treading softly, "that this is a bit more intense than kindergarten."

We all feel it, Mary Ellen thought. Everybody in this room knows that this love is on a different level. A deeper level.

Does that make it better? she wondered. Is it better to be more intense? Maybe it should scare me off. But I think it's drawing me nearer.

Impossible to imagine getting nearer to Pres! They were so close now that she felt one with him.

"We're happy for you," his mother said, setting the embroidery down, but still staring at her white French knots, still gripping her slender, silvery needle. "We're scared that you two are racing forward into something where — where you might get hurt. There's lots of time. Many years. Maybe you should ease up a little." Now she set the needle down and looked at each of them in turn. "Maybe you could calm down a bit. Back off."

They were not her parents. Mary Ellen waited for Pres's reply. But still he didn't scream or take offense. "We are racing. I admit it," said Pres. "But it's fun." He turned to her. "Isn't it?"

She could only nod.

Fun, definitely.

Tremendous, enveloping, terrific fun.

"I don't want either of you hurt," Mrs. Tilford said. "Sometimes you run that fast and somebody falls and — " She caught her breath. "Be careful of each other, you hear? No bruises. No spilled blood."

The teenagers laughed.

It could not happen to them. They would never have angry fights, or shout unprintable things, or be cruel to each other.

And Pres's parents sighed, because that was a part of being so much in love. To be sure that *you* won't have hard times; only other, poorly adjusted people do that. *Your* relationship will always be smooth.

Felicia Tilford, who knew all too well that money and looks and even love did not make life easy, ached for the two children on the couch.

No matter what Pres and Mary Ellen thought, there would be hard times ahead. Perhaps even vicious, hateful times.

But her son was in love, and it made her glad. It was, after all, what every mother wanted: to see her child happy.

And so she said no more, and neither did her husband.

CHAPTER 9

How few memories the basketball game brought back to Mary Ellen! She had seen all her basketball games as a cheerleader on the same level as the players: looking among the arms and legs of the team, looking up toward the baskets, up toward the fans, and up to the scoreboards. Now she sat above it all and farther back, and the game was surprisingly different. She saw it as more of a dance: Tarenton red and opposition blue weaving in and out in a prerehearsed pattern.

She sat with Pres, of course, and his parents, Avery, and Olivia's boyfriend, David Duffy. They were on the second from the top row opposite the Tarenton cheerleaders' side, not from choice but because they had arrived late and there were few seats left.

From across the gym the squad was simply a row of matching uniforms. Scarlet and white swayed and rose rhythmically. When the squad faced their own bleachers to shout, Mary Ellen could barely hear them; when they pivoted and faced across the gym, their voices rang strong through the squeak of sneakers and the shouts of fans.

They did not look like six individuals, but a team of shouts and pompons and colors.

It was what had always come hardest: being a team.

To push away their own desires and troubles. To be one of a group, working together. How hard it had been! And from what Olivia had told her, it was harder this year. Rarely did those six personalities jell.

But you would never know, Mary Ellen thought, filled with a nostalgic pride. You could not see any anger or in-fighting. You saw smiles and laughter. You heard cheers. You enjoyed the perfect tumbles and splits.

I must tell them, she thought, they are a success. They are a team. I hope they believe me.

Since Pres was talking to his mother, trying to explain the Tarenton defense tactics, Mary Ellen turned to chat with Avery. "Avery, you're hopeless. Look at you. Doing a page in *Games* magazine."

"I like *Games*. Look at the cover. Magazine for the super intelligent. Who could pass that up?" Avery said, grinning over his blunted pencil tip.

Mary Ellen laughed. "I have to pass that up. I

could only buy one that was called *Crosswords for the Totally Average.*"

It was Avery's turn to laugh. "Mary Ellen, you're all right," he said, which for him was the ultimate accolade.

She jabbed him sharply in the ribs. "Okay. Watch. Look up, quick. Hope's going to do something."

"What?" He looked around and saw nothing. "What's she going to do?"

"I don't know, but she's stepping away from the rest and getting herself ready for something."

Smallest of the six, she was a startling contrast in ice-white Varsity sweater and fair glowing skin. Hope sprang onto the suddenly bent backs of Tara and Olivia. The boys flanked this trio, doing nothing but looking terrific. Jessica, kneeling in front, leaped into the air. She came down in a dramatic split just as Hope back-flipped off the other girls and landed upright, arms flung out to touch fingertips with Sean and Peter.

The whole thing took but a few seconds.

It was breathtaking. People who had been watching the cheerleaders rather than the game burst into applause. People who had been watching the game looked around, startled, to see what deserved the round of applause.

"Wow. She's good," Avery said, going back to his puzzle.

"Just don't forget to tell her so," Mary Ellen ordered.

"Thanks, Mom. You help me with my manners, now," Avery said.

They both laughed.

All those months of isolation in New York and look at me now, Mary Ellen thought. She had a new set of friends and a new position in life so quickly. A wonderful, wonderful boyfriend; a good job; a fine seat at a fine game. They had shifted like players on a board: losing turns, passing GO, and gaining points.

I like my position here, she thought. I'm going to put it on HOLD and stay right here. For good.

"Would you ever want to be one again?" Pres asked suddenly.

"One what?"

Pres stared at her. "One cheerleader."

Wow, Mary Ellen thought. I have truly grown away. I am truly no longer a kid going to Tarenton High.

Pres grinned. "I guess not," he said, answering his own question. He took her hand and held it, looking at it, stroking it, and wishing they could be someplace private where he could hold Mary Ellen. "I'm moving in to the apartment day after tomorrow."

A place of his own, she thought. Her eyes went back to the white and scarlet row of Varsity Cheerleaders. No matter how sophisticated they thought themselves, they were kids. Pres Tilford was getting a place of his own.

Beside her, Avery shivered. Just going to work every day was hard enough, let alone getting your own place. To do your own laundry, mop your own floors, get your own groceries, swab out your own toilet? What horrible visions. Did

Pres realize that he was going to acquire a lot more than his own four walls? He was going to run up an awful lot of crummy chores.

You couldn't pay me, Avery Tilford thought.

How could his crazy cousin Pres, who set the clan standards for nutty behavior, be thinking in terms of buying a vacuum cleaner and a new set of china?

It was enough to make anybody throw up.

He was grateful to Hope for being in high school and having strict parents who would sooner Hope got typhoid than marry young.

Not me, Avery Tilford thought. He was so horrified he even found it necessary to move over a few inches so Pres's theories would not contaminate him.

Not *ever* me.

Tara felt the weight of Hope's little foot and enjoyed it. She loved the physical requirements of cheering. Bracing her body perfectly and keeping the exact arch that Hope needed, Tara's thoughts sprang into the air with Hope's body. She felt rather than saw the perfect landing, and she felt as much pride as Hope.

The squad whirled, came together, gave two final claps, and sat down in unison for a moment's rest on their bottom bleacher.

"Nice," the coach said without any enthusiasm.

Nice? Tara thought. It was terrific.

Directly into the small of Tara's back came the tip of another foot. Diana's. Although it was the worst possible location, because the spectators couldn't see the game whenever the cheerleaders were on their feet, Diana liked to sit as close to the squad as possible.

Tara nodded to let Diana know she felt the tap. She didn't dare turn to speak. Mrs. Engborg would yell at her. Better to have all the yelling directed at Olivia. Tara had a feeling Olivia could not take much more. Tara didn't want any more bad things to happen, but she kept toying with the idea of Olivia leaving the squad. It was like fussing with a lock of her hair: She kept curling the thought around in her mind.

If I were captain . . . Tara thought.

At that same moment, Olivia was dreaming.

If Gemma is right . . . if Mary Ellen and Pres are really in love . . . and he says he's getting a place of his own . . . what does that mean? Would she move in with him? Would her parents let her? Would they get married? At nineteen?

Gemma believed there would be a wedding.

Olivia would absolutely adore being in that wedding.

She didn't like thinking about marriage, really. Impossible to imagine marriage, somehow. But a wedding — that was perfectly possible. The perfect dress on the perfect day. Would Mary Ellen want Olivia in her wedding party? Were there all sorts of cousins and old, old friends Olivia didn't even know about who would be chosen as bridesmaids? What color would Mary Ellen want for gowns? Olivia did not care for pastels. They made her look like an invalid. But Mary Ellen leaned toward vibrant colors. Surely she'd want bridesmaids in colors like royal blue or golden yellow. But maybe that wasn't popular these days. Maybe Mary Ellen would wear ivory and the rest would be in pale, pale rose.

The game went on.

Olivia forgot about it.

Unexpectedly Tarenton made a basket. Olivia just sat there. The squad half stood, awaiting the cheer signal. Olivia just sat there. Mrs. Engborg glared at her. Olivia just sat there.

Tara smiled to herself. Leaping to her feet, she shouted, "Let's have a cheer for Wallace!" Her gestures told the rest of the squad what cheer she had chosen for Jimmy Wallace, and they leaped up to follow her.

"Way to go, Jim–my!" Tara screamed, doing a long, sweeping motion to her left. She crowded slightly onto Sean's territory, thus making it very difficult for Olivia to slip into the line.

There were a few moments of awkwardness, as the cooperating five of the squad shifted down. Even Jessica lost a beat moving over to let Olivia in. The cheer was badly done.

They bumped into each other sitting down, feeling stupid and not sure why, but resenting Olivia for not paying attention to the plays.

"Olivia," said Ardith Engborg, "in case you had not heard, it is the captain's task to notice what is going on and call the cheers."

Olivia flushed and licked her lips.

"Thank you, Tara," said Ardith sweetly. "We appreciate that *somebody* is following the basketball team."

"What if Jimmy Wallace had not gotten his cheer?" Ardith continued nastily.

It wouldn't have been the end of the world, Olivia thought, desperately trying not to cry.

Four of the squad looked away. Tara smiled at Olivia. Behind them both Diana smiled even more widely. Olivia muttered an apology.

I've been blaming Diana, she thought. But how can I do that? It really is all my fault. I'm sloppy. I'm lazy. I daydream. I goof off. I'm going to blame that on Diana? On Tara?

It's me. I'm no good.

The game went on. It was not exciting. Tarenton continued to keep a solid eight-point lead. When the game ended, the fans yelled momentarily and then clambered down the bleachers and left the gym. Now they had better things to do: get a pizza, go home and watch the news, brush their teeth. The game was history.

The cheerleaders stood in the empty room under the high ceilings while the noise and the crowds faded.

They knew they were in for yet another scolding, and they might as well stand together and get it over with.

Even the sight of her boyfriend coming to greet her did not raise Olivia's spirits. Now he'd hear this chewing out, too. It seemed to Olivia that David Duffy had heard nothing of her lately but bad things. She was incredibly depressed at the sight of his happy smile. What was he so happy about? Life was terrible. How was she going to break down and cry when he was obviously ready to go dancing?

Naturally, old Diana stood there looking beautiful and composed and capable. Naturally, Diana was talking softly to Mrs. Engborg, making friends with her, winning brownie points. Naturally, Diana, who even looked like Mary Ellen, would make a better captain than Olivia.

First, lady, you have to get on the squad, Olivia thought sullenly. I'm not giving up yet.

Pres came bounding out of the bleachers as if he were a one-man cheering squad. "Party!" he yelled, grinning from ear to ear and prancing like a puppy. "Party! Party! Everybody has to come!"

A party at Pres's mansion was always a treat. Even Olivia perked up slightly.

"Count me out," said Ardith. "Tired. Busy. Annoyed."

"Nope," Pres said. He picked up his former coach and held her by the waist in the air. The squad giggled. "You cannot be too busy for *me*," he told Ardith. "This is going to be the party of the week."

"Not interested. Set me down."

"The party of the month?" Pres offered.

"No. Set me down."

"Party of the year," Pres promised.

Ardith laughed. "Oh, well. In that case."

Pres set her down. He massaged his arm muscles and groaned loudly. "You have gained weight," he told her, falling down in exhaustion.

"Don't you know enough to stay in shape, woman?"

Ardith kicked him lightly. "I didn't gain an ounce. You are totally out of practice, boy."

Olivia slipped away to the locker room. Nice timing on Pres's part. Saved for another day.

Diana's cool eyes flickered as Olivia slid past. Olivia felt mousy and stupid and foolish.

Why am I even on this squad? she thought miserably. It's not fun. What's the point if I feel like I'm being tortured?

CHAPTER

The temperature had dropped. The wind picked up.

Snow fell thickly and the wind whipped it around the corners of Pres's house and drew it into drifts, disguising the bushes and trees.

The Tilfords turned on the floodlights. Even as their guests arrived at the mansion, the drive was being plowed again and the parking area opened up.

Across the lake, the twinkling lights of the houses on the opposite shore were barely visible through the snow. The lake itself no longer shone with ice, but was a soft field that stretched whitely, staying white even in the dark.

"Definitely," Pres said happily.

"Definitely what?" Mary Ellen asked.

"A snow fight."

"We will not. I'm wearing my good boots and stockings and long skirt."

"That's your problem," he said, grinning. He opened the door of the Porsche for her and waded into the snow to make a path for her. "I'm prepared. I have on wool socks, thick boots, jeans, and a ski jacket."

Tara, Sean, and Peter arrived in the next car. Sean was ready for action. "All right!" he yelled. "Let's divide into teams. I'm taking the lakeside. Here's the first one, Pres." He made a snowball and threw it accurately.

Given the breadth of Sean's shoulders and the muscles of his arms, it should have taken Pres's head off. But the snow wasn't packing well. It fell apart before it reached Pres.

"No problem," said Sean cheerily. "We'll just narrow the range." He closed in on Pres. Mary Ellen screamed, not wanting snow down her back. She raced through the snow up onto the enormous porch that encircled most of the house. She wasn't halfway there when her boots were entirely filled with snow. Lost cause, she thought. Laughing, she turned around and ambushed Sean.

"Hey!" he protested. "I thought you were safely inside."

"Never underestimate your enemy," Mary Ellen told him. She tried to give him an evil smile, but she was laughing too hard.

Olivia and David arrived. They joined Sean's team. Snowballs were flung fast and furiously. Since the snow refused to stay in balls, it was a highly unsuccessful war.

104

Nobody cared. They flung snow joyously, knocking each other over, leaping across the plump bushes, and hiding in the shadows, trying to catch an unprotected cheerleader.

Avery and Hope got out of his car and were immediately showered with snow. They took refuge behind the Porsche, planning a strategy that would get them indoors with the least possible snow on their bodies.

"You'll never make it!" Pres shouted. "We're all going to conspire against you!"

"Have a heart," Avery protested. "We are innocent bystanders in the great snowball fight of life."

"Nobody is innocent," Pres proclaimed. He raced alongside them and leaped into the air. Grabbing a huge branch of the towering fir tree, he swung from it, and dumped a load of snow down on Avery and Hope. Hope fell over, and Avery fell next to her.

Avery was furious. He detested little-kid horseplay. He did not want to have wet socks and a wet collar all evening just because his dumb cousin —

Not so dumb after all.

Wasn't Avery lying next to Hope? She was smiling.

The snow was insulating. They were warm next to each other.

"We need a code name for this military exercise!" Sean yelled.

Hope said, "How about Operation Blue Lips?"

Avery thought there would never be a better

line. "Cold lips?" he said to her, rolling closer.

Hope nodded as well as she could with her head in the snow.

Avery leaned over and kissed those lips for the first time. "Whew! They *are* cold."

"Frosted love," she said softly.

"I'm a defrost specialist," Avery told her.

They lay in the snow, laughing and hoping not to be stepped on.

Tara stood apart.

Jealousy that she could usually keep at bay overwhelmed her. Everybody seemed to be having such fun! And here she was, totally on the sidelines. Even though she loathed snow and did not want to be pelted, still she was very hurt that nobody had chosen her for a target. She might as well have been one of the trees for all the attention she was getting.

Sean went after Mary Ellen and Pres. Peter was basically going crazy, flinging stuff everywhere. Olivia and Duffy were being total nut cases, tossing snow the way little kids at the beach toss sand when their mothers aren't looking. And there lay Hope and Avery, sprawled in the snow for all the world, as if they were getting suntans.

I'm alone, Tara thought. She turned away when Avery kissed Hope. She wanted to go inside where it was warm. But if she went, she'd be the first. She'd feel dumb and even more out of it. Mr. and Mrs. Tilford were watching through the window, laughing. No doubt saying, "How cute — the kids are being kids again."

It isn't cute, Tara thought, filled to the brim with bad feelings. It's horrible.

She hated being left out. The whole point of being a cheerleader was that you *didn't* get left out. And here she was with her squad and people who were supposed to be her friends, and they had all forgotten she was alive.

Another car pulled up.

The shadow of the huge fir tree obscured it. Tara watched it for a moment. She recognized the passengers. And without letting herself think about the consequences, Tara shouted, "Olivia! I'll take the driver's side. You take the passenger side!"

Olivia was too excited to remember that all the teenagers had arrived by now. Resting three of her snowballs on the crook of her left arm, she opened fire the instant the passenger door cracked open.

Tara drifted back into the shadows.

A man she recognized as a science teacher got out of the driver's seat. Ardith Engborg clung to the door of the passenger side. She had on no hat, no scarf, and her coat was not zipped. Olivia's snowballs melted on her cheek, iced her throat, and plastered her hair.

"Oh!" Olivia said.

Ardith pushed through the snow and stared at the cheerleading captain. The snowball at her throat dripped down into her blouse and sweater. "I cannot believe you did this," Ardith said.

Olivia closed her eyes.

"I expect at least a *little* maturity from my *captain*."

"I'm sorry," Olivia whispered.

"I mean, do you think I am just one of the crowd?" the coach demanded. "Do you think I am another sophomoric, stupid, prank-playing, empty-headed — "

Mrs. Tilford came rushing down the path. "I'm *so* glad you came!" she panted. "All these children! Really, you must come in and give us some adult company, Ardith. We are absolutely *desperate*."

"I'll bet," Ardith said. "If this is the maturity level you live with around here — throwing snowballs at guests. . . ."

Mrs. Tilford put an arm around Ardith. "Well!" she said, probably because no other syllables came to mind. Ardith let herself be led in, and the science teacher trailed along. Olivia sent a sickly smile after them.

David Duffy came up to her. "Liv, you're having a hard time." He shook his head. "Got to get your act together, lady."

She began crying and turned away so he wouldn't see. "I'm trying! I'm trying!" she said. She wanted him to know how awful she felt — she wanted him to hug her and comfort her — and yet she felt too stupid to admit the depths of her despair.

I can't do anything right, she thought numbly. I can't be a captain, and I can't be a sensible young adult, I can't throw snowballs at the right people, and I can't even be a decent girl friend.

Olivia walked up the path into the house, David following her. She stepped into the prints of the coach's little feet. She wanted to go home. She had never felt in less of a party mood. They went up onto the wide veranda and stomped vigorously to shake the snow off before going in a side door. They kicked their boots off and headed into the enormous family room that faced the lake. Olivia was very relieved to hear the adults' voices coming from the formal living room on the far side of the house.

By now it was too cold out for the rest, and very soon the whole crowd was indoors. Mary Ellen's cheeks were apple red from the wind, and her golden hair had slipped from its braids and hung in thin tendrils around her face. Pres could not take his eyes off her. It was such a burden to be the host! To worry about who had a soda and who didn't, to hang up coats and speak pleasantries! All he wanted was to be alone with Mary Ellen.

Patrick and Jessica, who had come around the front way and missed the entire snowball fight, already had the best places by the roaring fire. With the assurance of a best friend, Patrick was host along with Pres. Patrick chose a few tapes so they'd have music, and turned the volume up until the room pulsed with rock.

The music made talk impossible.

Olivia was just as glad; she felt too down for cheerful patter. Tara didn't mind. Nobody was talking to her, anyway, and now it was not so obvious. Jessica almost held her ears. All night they had screamed at the game, while around them feet pounded bleachers, and fans shrieked, and referees' whistles screamed. Now she had to endure more music?

Instead of calming her, the music made Jessica want to abandon the party.

As for Hope and Avery, they did abandon it. Avery had lived with the Tilfords for a month now and he knew every corner of the mansion. The little-used front hall was where he led Hope. Here the stairs rose dramatically, with two landings instead of one, and at the second was a narrow window seat. Soft cushions, sat on by nobody but the Persian cat when the sun came through the window, had always attracted Avery. But he had not previously had anyone to share the window seat with.

Peter watched them go. He didn't really follow them, but he drifted down the hall to see where they went. He heard their low laughter as they turned past the first landing.

My girl friend, he thought. Some girl friend.

He turned around and leaned against the doorframe, pretending to be surveying the party.

Sean knew better. "Go after her if you like her that much."

"I'm not going to fight for somebody. Nobody matters that much."

Sean shrugged. "Nobody matters that much to me, but you sure are moping around these days."

"I am not moping," Peter said sharply.

He knew perfectly well he was moping. He'd liked it with Hope. She demanded little . . . he gave little. Nice, easy relationship. Well, he had learned one thing. Hope didn't want an easy relationship. She wanted to be with Avery, who gave a lot . . . and probably intended to take a lot.

Bet Avery gets along fine with the Changs, too, Peter thought. He had never done well with Hope's stiff, difficult family. Never tried, really, because he felt he should not have to try. They should automatically like him the way he came. And Hope should, too.

Tara came up to the two boys. "Dance with me," she said. There was no uplift to her voice — it was in no way a question. She was giving them orders. She expected to be danced with. It was their job.

Sean liked Tara a lot and he felt like dancing. But he believed Peter could use a little female attention right now. Nobody could take Peter's mind off Hope like Tara. Sean smiled and said nothing and did not reach for Tara's waist and hand to dance with her.

Peter definitely did not feel like dancing. He felt like socking Avery Tilford in the mouth and dragging Hope off somewhere and telling her how he *really* felt. The only thing that stopped him was that he didn't *know* how he really felt.

So neither one of them danced with Tara.

She pretended to laugh.

Pretended to have fun.

But all evening her heart burned with loneliness, and with jealousy.

* * *

An hour into the party Mary Ellen found herself alone with Mrs. Tilford. Somebody had turned the music down and conversation was at last possible. People had drifted about the house. She hadn't seen Hope and Avery in quite a while; Jessica and Patrick were out in the snow building an enormous snowman, and Sean and Tara had gone out to help them. Olivia and Duffy were dancing slowly. Pres had been sent to shovel snow away from Ardith's car so she could leave.

"I went over to see Pres's apartment," Mrs. Tilford said. "It's lovely. He's going to be happy there."

Mary Ellen smiled. "Yes, I think so." She could feel Mrs. Tilford's hesitation. She knew Pres's mother was wondering what Mary Ellen's plans were. Had her son and this girl talked about the possibility of living together? Were they still young enough for Mrs. Tilford to make rules and insist on certain standards? Or were they adults and she would simply have to live with the decisions that Mary Ellen and Pres made?

Mary Ellen had considered their living together. But it wasn't what she wanted. She was beginning to believe that Pres was what she wanted, but she would pass on moving in with him.

It was her parents' marriage Mary Ellen thought of. How did the marriage vows go? *For better or for worse, for richer or for poorer, in sickness and in health.*

It had not been an easy life for the Kirkwoods. They had consistently been worse, been poorer,

112

and been sick. Yet they had remained in love, held hands, and been a comfort to each other.

Mary Ellen wanted to say those vows herself. Out loud, in front of her friends and family, she wanted to promise those same things, and know that when push came to shove, she, Mary Ellen, would be there for the long haul.

Living together.

It didn't sound like a long haul. Whatever she did, it would be forever.

"Are you happy with your day-care job?" Mrs. Tilford asked.

"Yes. I love little kids. I have the newborns. The center doesn't take them until they're eight weeks old, and I'm in charge of four little teeny babies. They're adorable."

This obviously put Mrs. Tilford in a panic. How much did Mary Ellen love babies? Enough to want one of her very own? With Pres?

Mary Ellen said hastily, "But eight hours a day is plenty, you know. I get to give them back to their mothers then."

Mrs. Tilford was visibly relieved. They chatted about babies for a while, a topic Mrs. Tilford had not considered since Pres was out of diapers. Then she said, "We'd like to have your parents over for dinner, Mary Ellen. Mr. Tilford and I want to get to know them better. So I thought I'd call and see if they can join us one evening next week."

Her father was a bus driver. He was not a talker, and rarely said much to his passengers except, "Nice day" or, if it suited, "Terrible day."

Her mother was a clerk, whose life was very bound up in office gossip and in a cooking club to which she belonged, and whose favorite activity was going to tag sales, scrounging secondhand household objects.

You could say all you wanted about America having no class structure, but the Kirkwoods were divided from the Tilfords by many enormous gulfs. By sophistication, by money, by travel and lack of it, by education, and by social preference.

Felicia Tilford had been president of the Junior League for years, and now headed the historical society. She raised tens of thousands of dollars for the hospital auxiliary, wore fur coats, traveled routinely to Europe, flew often to college and sorority reunions, and played bridge.

That should be an interesting evening. Her parents and the Kirkwoods.

Her parents were going to be nervous wrecks. Her mother would not have a thing to wear, and her father would not have a thing to say.

And Mary Ellen knew that she had become an adult, because it did not upset her. She loved her mother and father. The Tilfords would have to love them, too, and that was that.

"That would be lovely," Mary Ellen said. "What night did you have in mind?" She guessed Tuesday. Mondays and Wednesdays Mrs. Tilford had her club meetings. Thursdays they never missed the country club, because it was the night their particular crowd always dined there. Fridays and Saturdays either they entertained or were entertained, or they went out of town to do something truly exciting.

"I was hoping for Thursday," said Mrs. Tilford. "We'd all go to the club and have a lovely evening."

Mary Ellen was truly amazed. No private little dinner? They were going to march right out in front of all their distinguished friends and eat at the country club?

What had Pres said to his parents to make Felicia Tilford decide on this? Had Pres given them orders? Had he told them —

What could he have told them?

All his crazy proposals of marriage. . . .

Is he serious? Mary Ellen thought. Did he say to his mother, "You'd better get to know her parents because they're going to be my in-laws"?

Mary Ellen stared into Felicia Tilford's eyes.

For the first time she really seriously considered becoming Mary Ellen Tilford. Mrs. Preston Tilford III.

They were no longer Pres's mother and a blonde cheerleader in the same room. They were two women looking nervously at a future they could not quite see, and feeling their way toward the right thing.

It won't happen, Mary Ellen thought. Pres? A few weeks alone in that apartment, being a wild bachelor, and he'll toss out the idea of marriage. Pres — married? Hah. Maybe ten years from now.

Pres walked back in.

Snow was melting in his dark blond hair.

Mary Ellen wanted to run to him and brush it away, smooth his hair down, and stay next to him — stay forever.

How much do I love this boy? she thought, not moving. How does a girl know? What tells you that you love a person enough to get married? Do you get a sign in the night? Or do you just tremble and plunge in?

CHAPTER

Jessica was so surprised to be there.

She didn't feel ready to be this grown-up.

How could Pres feel ready? How could Pres — who, at times, was the most childish of them all — be launching himself into adulthood so completely? How could it be Pres who had rented this apartment, and was now proudly showing off the stereo system he had just bought to Patrick and Jessica? Showing them where he had experimented placing the two large speakers?

Trust Pres to buy a stereo system before he thought of buying a mop. The place was distinctly in need of a good sweeping and dusting. Jessica looked covertly at Mary Ellen. Was Mary Ellen yearning to wield a broom in here? Yuck. Cleaning house, however, seemed to be the furthest thing from Mary Ellen's mind.

" 'Course it's a little lonely at breakfast," Pres said, "but once Mary Ellen and I get married, it won't be."

Jessica gasped.

"Oh, *Pres*," Mary Ellen said, laughing. "He's just being silly," she told Jessica. "He loves to joke about marriage. He doesn't mean a thing. He intends to go out with eighty hundred girls this year and be a swinging bachelor."

"I did all that," Pres said. "I was precocious. Finished that up by high school graduation. Now I'm ready for real life."

Mary Ellen rolled her eyes and laughed again.

Jessica picked up the cue and laughed also.

Neither boy laughed.

Uh-oh, Jessica thought. "Well!" she said brightly. "It was great of you to take us through the apartment, Pres. I'm honored."

Pres snorted. "You make it sound like a museum tour."

It had felt like a museum tour. An exhibit of what Jessica's life might be like five or ten years from now, when she'd finished college and had been working a while. But now — at nineteen? Jessica was horrified. She would no more do this than sign up to be an astronaut.

Mary Ellen's fingers strayed over the back of the couch. "I envy you, Pres," she said. "I'd like getting out of my house. Have some space of my own. Room for me, and my things, and my plans."

How Jessica could identify with that! Ever since her mother's remarriage, the house had not been big enough. She never really wanted to be around her stepfather. She scooted quickly up stairs, hiding in her room, eating dinner faster than she'd like in order to escape the man. But you could never really be away from somebody who lived under the same roof.

More and more Jessica thought of college, and how wonderful it would be to go away. *Really* away. None of this local state university for her. She wanted hundreds of miles between them, so there was no possibility she could come home on a weekend. She could legitimately separate herself from her family and from Tarenton and not even feel guilty. Mary Ellen had been separated for a while. She hadn't stuck it out. Why? Jessica wondered. Fear of failure? Genuine failure? Homesickness?

Or love of Preston Tilford?

Jessica didn't want any heart-to-heart talks. The whole romance made her shrink in on herself. Mary Ellen might be old enough for marrying, but she, Jessica, was not. Jessica would almost rather repeat junior high than hear a proposal of marriage.

So naturally, when she and Patrick left, went down the stairs, and came out through the empty garages and into the bright sun, when Jessica was busy squinting into the glare of sun on snow and rummaging in her purse for her sunglasses — naturally Patrick proposed to her.

Oh, not straight out. The words weren't, "Jessica, will you marry me?" But he said, "I'd love to do that. Have a place of my own. I guess some guys need years to grow up," Patrick said. "College, the army, all that. But I grew up fast, Jessica. I want what Pres has."

Quickly Jessica headed for Patrick's van, getting there first and opening her door herself, and sliding in. Patrick caught up and closed the door softly, with a finality that made Jessica shudder. She wrapped her coat around her as if she needed protection. Patrick walked around, got in, and shut his door the same way: a thick, solid closing.

Like the future, Jessica thought, suffocating in the car.

She rolled down the window in spite of the icy wind, feeling panic. Life would shut her in like those two doors.

"Jessica, I want to get serious," Patrick said.

"No."

"I love you, Jessica."

He didn't attempt to touch her. She leaned against her door instead of against him, and did not look his way. "Patrick, it isn't for me. Not now and maybe never. I can't look into Mary Ellen's heart, or Pres's, or even yours. But I can look into mine. No matter how much I like you, I am not going to get serious. Whatever that means. Serious is *wrong*. Serious is *crazy*. We're *kids*."

"But, Jessica — "

"No 'but Jessica.' I will not talk about it and I will not listen to you talk about it. Start the engine; let's get going."

"Where do you want to go?" he said, starting the van obediently. It caught quickly. She felt safer with that noise under them, as if it could pad the harsh words she had just had to say. She didn't know where she wanted to go. Not home. She wanted to do something fun with Patrick. He was the best company she'd ever had. But he would ruin things. He would want to imitate Pres: talk about apartments and getting serious and settling down and all that.

"I'm hungry," he said. "Want a hamburger?"

"Sure."

Jessica tried to think only of hamburgers and pickles, french fries, and thick strawberry shakes. It began to work. She relaxed and felt cold and hungry.

"Please, Jessica, let's talk about it," Patrick tried once more. "I want you to know how I feel. It's so much more important than you are allowing it to be, Jessica. It's our future together. I don't know why you're always afraid of the future. I would never let a single thing — "

"Stop the car," Jessica said.

He stared at her.

Jessica, who never yelled except when cheering, yelled, *"Stop — the — van!"*

He stopped the van, shocked.

"I'm getting out," she said, her hand on the door handle. "I'm going over to Tara's. She lives down this block. She'll take me home when I'm ready. You go have your hamburger. We're finished."

He said nothing, just looked at her.

"Patrick." She was fighting tears and fighting rage. "This is what I'm serious about. I'm serious

121

about being a high school senior. About having fun my last year at home. About having a good time when I'm with you. I'm serious about being seventeen years old and doing what other seventeen-year-olds do. If you want to share that with me, fine."

He was very still. His eyes were on her, but clouded over. Unfocused. Jessica could not imagine Patrick Henley weeping. "And if you want a different kind of serious, Patrick, the kind that spells engagement and marriage and apartments and car payments — forget it. I won't play. Find some other girl, somebody who's ready for that. Because I'm not."

She was being too dramatic. She was faintly ashamed of herself. But she got out and shut the door hard — much harder than he had. The van rocked slightly. She stepped over a dirty gray mass of packed snow at the edge of the road and into the narrow pedestrian way beyond it. Nobody had shoveled. Roughly packed by the soles of many boots, it had iced over and was narrow, rutted, and treacherous. Jessica walked very carefully. She did not look back. Behind her the engine of Patrick's van did not change beat, did not shift into first and drive away, did not follow her, and did not leave.

She kept walking toward Tara's.

What am I doing? she thought.

I am throwing away a boy who truly loves me. A boy who really could take me away from a difficult family situation and put me in a much better one. How often in my life will I meet a boy who wants to do that? Or who can? Who will ever love me more than Patrick? Will I ever meet a man I will love more, either?

She almost turned.

At the intersection, when she looked both ways for traffic, she almost looked back to Patrick, still idling at the edge of the road.

She thought if she crossed this street she would never have Patrick again, not at all. His pride would not allow it. He would date another girl. Her senior year would be ruined — lonely and desperate and agonizing.

And she was going to Tara's? She wasn't close to Tara. She would have to spill details of this to Tara, of all people. And yet, curiously, she wanted a girl to talk to, and, in the end, she thought she could probably rely on Tara.

She stared blindly at the road. Cross? Or run back to Patrick?

She crossed the street and walked down two houses and rang the bell at Tara's. Tara opened the door, blinked in amazement, and let her in. What Patrick did, or where he went, Jessica did not know.

CHAPTER

 12

It was Tara's idea to go up to Deer Park for a day. Tarenton had lakes and rinks, so Tarenton kids didn't often make the long drive up to the sports playground. But Jessica seized on it. If they went in a big group, the next time she dealt with Patrick would be in a crowd, ever so much easier on both of them. The rest of the cheerleaders had cabin fever from the long winter and were thrilled at the whole idea, and immediately they had three carloads ready to spend Saturday on snow and ice.

Saturday dawned in perfect weather. The sky was blue, not the grim, slate blue of winter, but a soft, happy blue, like spring. There was no wind, so although the temperature was still low, they felt warm in the sunlight. They could unzip jackets, forget scarves, and peel off layers as the sun rose in the sky.

Snow still lay on the ground. It was melting rapidly along the roadsides and paths. Slush puddles and ice made walking difficult and driving messy.

Mary Ellen wanted to rent a horse-drawn sleigh. She'd snuggle under a fur rug next to Pres while the sleighbells rang and the horses whinnied. Then they'd have hot chocolate before a blazing fire in the main lounge of Deer Park.

Sean wanted to ice-fish or rent an iceboat with Peter. Peter was trying to find somebody sufficiently daredevil to go on a bobsled with him. The rest were willing to toboggan down one of the packed runs, but bobsled speed was a bit too much for them.

Patrick was asking both Tara and Jessica to rent cross-country skis and circle the woods with him. Hope and Avery were beginning to be sorry they'd come. "I am not the type for any of the above-named activities," Avery said uneasily. He didn't want to look like a jerk in front of Hope. It was easy to shrug off basketball when he was sitting in the bleachers, but it was going to be very tough to shrug off anything now that he was part of a sports party.

"There's plenty to do indoors," Jessica said. "We came up last year and we . . . well . . . well — " She broke off. It had not been a successful trip. Trying to make a warm and loving family had never been successful for the five of them. Jessica's two older brothers remained obstinately silent the entire eight hours of the excursion. Her stepfather was consistently tense. Her mother got frantic and nervous. Jessica merely endured. "I played Trivial Pursuit in the main lounge," Jessica told Avery. "They were having a tournament. You drew a number and got added to a team. It was fun."

"You played with strangers?" Hope asked dubiously.

"They weren't strangers by the time we'd lost four games in a row," Jessica said, laughing. "Anyway the main lounge has indoor activities if you're sick of the snow. So you two super athletes had better head there."

Hope had no idea what to do. She'd invited Avery, but Avery didn't really want to be there, and Peter was glaring at her because Avery was there.

Peter had slipped from her mind so fast it was embarrassing. Their relationship must have dwindled to nothing for Avery to replace Peter in her affections so completely and so swiftly. But Peter was not saying or doing anything to get her back, just looking annoyed and sort of pouting, like a kid.

"I remember now why I came," Avery said very softly. Over the music from the car radio she could barely hear him. She leaned closer, which was obviously what Avery had in mind, because he smiled. What a lovely smile he had!

"Why?" she said.

"To be with you."

They hugged spontaneously and laughed under their breath. Hope forgot Peter completely.

In the front seat there was a remarkable distance between driver and passenger. Patrick was making himself drive with both hands on the wheel, which took considerable concentration, since he had driven for many months now with one hand wrapped around Jessica's. Jessica was busily looking out the window announcing the sights. There weren't many out in the woods, so she was reduced to saying things like, "Look at that motel," and, "My, what tall pines."

I'm lucky, Patrick told himself. I get to be with her. I have to be grateful for that. I have to be polite and a stranger. When she and Tara and I go skiing, the only circumstance under which I can touch Jessica is if she falls down and can't get up after two tries. Then I can hold her hand till she's on her feet. Give her a casual smile and ski on.

Oh, yeah, I'm real lucky. Definitely. This is just the way my master plan for life was meant to be. Friends. Jessica tells me this morning when we cram ourselves into this car that she wants to be just friends now.

Let's not date, Patrick. Let's just be friends. We're going on this trip to Deer Park. Let's just be friends in a crowd. I'm not your girl friend and you're not my boyfriend; we're just plain old friends.

Friends rot, Patrick thought. I hate being friends. I am morally opposed to being just friends.

Jessica said brightly, "I wore my ice-skating

outfit under my jeans. While you're cross-country skiing with Tara, I think I'll do a little figure skating, Patrick."

A good thing his hands were on the wheel. It gave him something to strangle.

In Sean's car, right behind them, things were slightly better. Sean was happy, anyway. He liked ice-fishing and he liked ice-boating and he could do them alone, or with a buddy, or with strangers, and it didn't matter at all. Ahead of them in the backseat of Patrick's car, Hope and Avery hugged each other. Peter fumed helplessly. Sean pretended he hadn't seen a thing.

Tara sat between Peter and Sean. Sitting between two boys was the nicest thing she could imagine, but not these two at this particular moment. Peter had yet to notice her, he was so annoyed about Avery and Hope. And Sean was all wrapped up in his driving and when he talked it was of ice-fishing, which Tara thought sounded about as uncomfortable an activity as had ever been invented. She wanted to be up there with Jessica and Patrick, arranging their cross-country skiing. It had been a real sacrifice not to sit with them in their car. Because either Jessica and Pat would get back together, in which case she would have been a great friend to help Jessica through that, and that would increase her popularity — or Jessica and Patrick would *not* get back together, in which case she would be right there to attract Patrick just when he needed a friend himself.

Either way, a winner.

But no, she was sitting with Sean and Peter.

She would have preferred to go to Deer Park in the evening. They had fantastic dances at night in the main lounge. Massive fires blazed at either end of the great room, and college boys filled the floor and the dancing went on till dawn. But no, they were going by day when the place would be full of little kids and their mothers and fathers.

Behind her Olivia and David Duffy snuggled. It was a very unfair world where other people got to snuggle and she, Tara, was isolated. I'm alone again, she thought. Why do I keep believing I can arrange things to suit myself? She stared at her reflection in the window. She was very pretty. She liked her looks. Liked her hair and her nose and her figure and her eyes. So why didn't this help her get what she wanted? What was the point in looking good when nobody noticed?

Oh, well, she could cross-country ski, which she liked, and even if Patrick and Jessica didn't speak to each other the whole way, it should be sort of fun, maybe.

At the entrance gate, the eleven of them paid their fees and then stood there, slightly unsure. They were reluctant to split off into small groups when they had only just come.

"Why don't we all skate for a while?" Mary Ellen suggested. "We'll go out on Family Lake, and we can play tag. Or flick the whip."

"Whip!" Sean yelled immediately. "I love to flick the whip."

The rest groaned. But they wanted to do something together and even Avery, who could scarcely stand on skates, said he'd try. "I'll be the pivot of the whip," said Sean," and you'll be next, Avery. I'll keep you on your feet and the second person to catch your arm will support you on the other side. No problem."

"I'll be the second person," Hope said instantly, beaming.

Peter glared at her. Nobody noticed.

"Great," Avery moaned. "Somebody as tiny as you are has to hold me up."

"Aaaah, by the time she catches up, you'll be an expert," Sean told him.

They rented their skates and tied them tightly, sitting on a log by the front of Family Lake. Speed skaters and figure skaters went elsewhere, so early in the day this spot had few skaters; but it would fill up later with people just wanting to have fun. Avery was relieved to see people falling down all over the ice. Still, he was not looking forward to the first time he fell down.

As it happened, he fell before he even got onto the ice.

"Don't skate much, do you?" Peter observed.

"Don't skate at all," Avery said. He barely knew Peter. He did not even know Peter had been Hope's boyfriend, because Hope had not mentioned him, and his cousin Pres was much too involved with Mary Ellen to think of bringing up anybody else's romantic life.

Sean hauled Avery up.

Avery was very impressed. Sean was truly strong. If that was what cheerleading did for a fellow. . . . "Nah," Sean said. "I lift weights. I do a lot of sports. Skiing, tennis, sailing. I use my muscles in cheerleading, but I develop them elsewhere."

"Must we spend our whole day discussing your physique?" Tara said.

"What better subject?" Sean asked.

Pres was kneeling in front of Mary Ellen, lacing up her skates. She was wearing dark blue pants and a scarlet jacket, and her blonde hair was framed against those bright colors. "Let's talk about marrying Mary Ellen instead," he said brightly. He drew himself up on one knee, clasped his hands before Mary Ellen in a dramatic, begging posture, and cried, "Mary Ellen! Will you marry me? Say yes, say yes!"

It was loud enough for half the skaters to hear. The rest of the group giggled nervously. Mary Ellen just laughed. "You nut. Get up and skate."

Pres beamed a crazy, teenage grin at the rest. "At least she didn't turn me down this time," he said, rolling his eyes and blinking rapidly like a clown. "Progress. I'm moving right along. Maybe I should set the wedding date now."

"Maybe you should skate your brains out," Mary Ellen said.

"Don't you have faith in my brains?" Pres said mournfully. They teased each other nonstop, holding hands as they moved out onto the ice. They were playing to an audience, but they were, at the same time, entirely alone, entirely together.

Sean had almost been ready to ask Tara to

rent an iceboat with him after they played flick the whip. Now he didn't think he wanted a girl's company all that much. Normally Pres was a good guy, but right now he was abnormal. All this talk about marriage was beginning to get to Sean. Marriage? Was Pres mentally ill?

Sean skated off quickly.

"Now how am I supposed to catch him?" Avery said. "He goes off at a hundred miles an hour and I'm crawling over the ice."

"We'll get him for you!" Pres cried. Linking arms with Mary Ellen, he flashed after Sean. Avery tottered to his feet a second time. Peter made a point of skating gracefully in circles around Avery, while Avery's ankles bent and the skates angled outward and Avery fell over again.

"I'll say this for you," Tara said, laughing, "you sure are a good sport, Avery." Hooking an elbow through Avery's right arm while Hope took his left, they got him upright and began guiding him out to where Pres and Mary Ellen had captured Sean.

"Crack the whip is fun," Tara told Avery. "You're going to love it."

"I doubt it," Avery panted. He tried standing still, feet pointed ahead, so that when the girls skated, they towed him along. This worked nicely until his toes began to point out and his legs began spreading. He lost his balance, tumbled over backward and pulled both girls down with him. They screamed because they liked screaming. Olivia and Duffy helped them up. "I want to thank you for being here," Duffy told Avery.

132

"This is a first for me. Today, in comparison to you, I am a super athlete."

"Good," Avery said. "I like having a purpose in life."

For nearly an hour they played crack the whip. Sean's strength made him an excellent pivot, and Jessica loved being the very last skater who had to try to catch up with the rapidly whirling line. They fell over so much that Sean wanted to meet later in the sauna and compare bruises.

Avery said, "This place is sufficiently civilized to have a sauna?"

"It's not coed," Patrick told him.

"Oh, well then. Forget it."

The day flew by.

In the end, they stayed in a group.

It was not a group that had ever been together in quite that way before. It was nine people revolving around two. Avery and Hope were beginning to get close, but this day they were still really strangers. Olivia and Duffy had been close for a long time, but yet their relationship was relatively casual. Jessica and Patrick were practicing distance, and the rest were singles.

But Pres and Mary Ellen were a unit. Their jokes were for each other only. Their eyes were glued to each other. They touched constantly, laughed over nothing, and hugged every few moments. Twice more Pres asked Mary Ellen to marry him and twice more she giggled. "No, you crazy man. But I'll have some hot chocolate."

Sean said in an undertone to Peter, "Sick."

"What is?"

"Pres."

"Lovesick, that's for sure."

"Spare me," Sean said. That variety of illness was one he could do without.

Hope said softly to Avery. "Is your cousin serious?"

Avery shrugged. "I never thought Pres had the capacity to be serious about anything. But then I don't know him as well as you Tarenton kids do. Maybe he is."

Hope blinked, shivering.

Avery grinned. "I agree. I cannot imagine signing away my future on the dotted line at our age. But they might. Just might."

As for Olivia, she could not take her eyes off Mary Ellen and Pres. Come on, Melon, say yes! she thought. He's really and truly asking you. He really and truly wants to marry you. Say yes! I want to be in a wedding.

Jessica listened to the silly proposals and wondered if Pres wanted a marriage or a wedding. A wedding, Jessica thought, is a great, big, wonderful party. Everybody loves a wedding. But marriage. Marriage is tough stuff. I've seen a bad marriage or two. Does Pres really want marriage?

Jessica studied Pres.

She studied Mary Ellen.

She didn't find any answers.

But she had an answer of her own. To Patrick she would never say yes.

CHAPTER

There was an early thaw. The snow melted very quickly now. Slush puddles filled the sidewalks and streets until walking became impossible. Mud was everywhere. For a few days Tarenton was simply ugly, with grimy, old snow vanishing into brown, muddy ground. Everybody grumbled. Real winter, with thick ice and deep snow, was much, much better than this useless half winter, they complained.

At work it seemed to Mary Ellen all the children either had bad colds or were coming down with the flu. At the factory it seemed to Pres all the employees were irritable, unable to concentrate.

School did not change. Tarenton won another basketball game and lost another. Jessica aced an exam and Tara failed it. Hope played her violin for Avery, and Avery's college wrote back to say he could try again in September.

Overnight, the temperature fell a good thirty degrees. In the morning the mud was rock-hard. The only snow left was the tiny remains of once-impressive snowmen.

At ten on a school-day morning, the sun came out. Inside the classroom the heat built up. Heads turned to stare yearningly at the sky and the sun, and spring fever hit the entire school population at the same moment.

At lunch, they ignored the cafeteria. By the dozens they ran into the courtyard to sit on the long granite benches. A group of kids carried their radios onto the soccer field and began dancing. Jessica wandered toward the dancers, eating an ice-cream sandwich.

"Where did you get that?" exclaimed Tara.

"Cafeteria. I think they've had it on the shelf since last summer and it melted and refroze at least weekly." She bit down on soft vanilla and crunchy chocolate wafer. "Mmmmmm. I don't care how stale it is. What a taste, after this long winter!"

"Ooooh, let me have a bite," Tara begged.

"Sure."

Tara nibbled. "Winter's almost over," she said happily. "I am in the mood for love. Let's fall in love, Jessica."

Jessica did not even bother to answer that, but Tara hardly noticed. "Let's ask Ardith if we can have cheerleading practice outside," Tara went on. "I have never felt so cooped up."

Tara flung her arms out into the spring, as if hugging the soft air. She danced alone to the music coming from the kids out on the soccer field. Jessica danced alone, too, but for her it was by choice, and that made all the difference.

It was not just the cheerleaders who begged to stay outdoors. The Pompon Squad sat on the football field bleachers, facing the sun, pretending they were starting their tans. They had only two maneuvers to practice, and they just sat there yelling joyfully and waving their scarlet and white pompons and banners.

The marching band had been sitting indoors on gray folding chairs for months. Now they could march again. Stepping high from the sheer pleasure of being in the fresh air, they covered the field with precision steps and turns, obeyed signals, and played John Philip Sousa.

Both boys' and girls' basketball teams warmed up outside. Slowly, they did laps around the entire playing field area, skirting the football field, the soccer field, the baseball diamond, and the tennis courts.

At the edge of the blacktop parking lot for teachers stood the cheerleaders.

They chatted more than they worked, and for once Ardith Engborg didn't yell at them; she had spring fever perhaps even worse than they did.

Not many students caught the bus home. They heard the band playing and the squads shouting, and they drifted out behind the school and couldn't bring themselves to leave. By the score

137

they wandered through the athletic teams and up onto the empty bleachers, and sat flirting and talking and staring into the sky.

At three, Pres finished up at the factory and drove immediately to pick up Mary Ellen at the day-care center. As full of spring fever as anyone, she was waiting by the curb.

How lovely she looked! Pres could hardly stand it. She was wearing a skirt with knee socks and a large, softly draped white blouse. The sweater she normally pulled on to cover the blouse was tied over her shoulders. Her hair was loose and ruffled in the wind. Over her arm was her heavy winter coat, held as if she'd never need to wear it again.

She hopped in the car and then leaned very, very slowly toward him for a kiss, and they kissed gently, as if matching the weather. "Marry me?" Pres said, his words muffled by the fact that he continued kissing her.

Without moving her lips, Mary Ellen shook her head and the kiss went on.

They parted an inch, took a breath, and kissed again.

"Please?" Pres said.

Mary Ellen shook her head and kissed him a third time, very briskly, ending the subject. "What are we doing today?"

"Let's go over to the high school. When I drove by everybody was outside. Celebrating the season, I guess."

Mary Ellen had no desire to go to the high school. But she couldn't think of anything she really wanted to do, so she said that would be nice, and settled in for the short drive.

Instead of parking in front, Pres drove around to the football field parking lot. Gravel spurted under his tires and he steered around slush puddles. A dozen kids waved at them, recognizing the Porsche.

Pres parked on purpose so that when Mary Ellen opened her door she'd look down into two inches of ice water. Grinning, he walked around, put his hands on his hips and said, "Guess I'd better carry you."

"Pres, sometimes you get so silly I'm embarrassed."

"Go on. You love it." He didn't carry her. He caught her as she leaped off the rim of the car and they both ran toward the bleachers. "The very top," Pres said, hauling her up and up and up.

"It'll be too breezy up there," she protested. "Let's sit down with all the other kids and — "

"No. We're not all the other kids. We're *us.*"

That was true. So they sat on top, so close they were lopsided. Pres wrapped her coat around them both because she was right, it was windy on the top row. They huddled, with affection and cold, and soaked up the weak sunlight.

"How pretty it is," Mary Ellen said. Nobody was in uniform. No cheerleaders in scarlet and white. No marching band with gold epaulets, no drill corps with banners. And yet the groups formed a perfect picture: a painting for a greeting card full of joy and energy and sound. She told Pres all of this.

"You're just in love," he said. "You think everything is perfect because you're in love with me."

She stared at the figures of the high school students. Only a year ago she had been among them. "Yes," she said at last. "I am in love."

They looked at each other. There was no kissing, there was no talking. They tried to see into the eyes of the other, to find the answers to their questions, but eyes tell nothing. Only words and actions can speak. Mary Ellen choked with emotion and had to look away. Pres held her tightly, but did not interrupt her thoughts with another marriage proposal. If he asked me now, would I say yes? she thought. Oh, Pres, let me sit here in the sun and try to figure out who I am. Whether you and I should be *one*. Don't speak. Just hold me tight.

The teams practiced. Shouts rang around the field. The John Philip Sousa march was piercingly loud as the band faced them, and vanished into an echo when the band turned away. The bass drums made the ground tremble, and the piccolo shrilled constantly.

A small plane appeared.

At first it was as small as a soaring bird, a point in the blue sky. The sun caught the metal and as the plane tilted, the metal glinted and Mary Ellen blinked. She thought the plane seemed exceptionally long and thin in comparison to its wingspan, as if it had a tail.

Next to her, Pres's body was the most warm and comforting presence she had ever known. This is where I want to be, she thought. I think there *is* an "us." I think the day will come when —

It was just advertising: huge letters strung out behind the plane.

Mary Ellen smiled. What a sign of spring! You could advertise like that only when there were crowds of people outdoors to read it. She didn't think she had ever seen a plane attempt this so early in the spring. Probably for new cars. Low interest rate, or something. Possibly a new restaurant was opening. She and Pres would make a point to go there.

The marching band halted.

The band director pointed at the little plane.

Clarinets and trombones, flutes and snare drum sticks — all were slowly lowered. Nearly a hundred band members stared up at the advertising.

The plane was coming directly toward Pres and herself, so Mary Ellen could not quite make out the words. She could see the letter R and the letter M repeated, but the words remained a mystery.

The cheerleaders on the blacktop began screaming insanely.

Mary Ellen stared at them. They were not cheering. They were leaping up and down like untrained first-graders getting a big treat.

It must be quite a restaurant, Mary Ellen thought. Perhaps they're offering some prize. A trip to Hawaii or something. But how much information could be included on a short strip of letters?

Puzzled, she looked up again.

The sky was very blue and very clear.

The plane was silver.

The letters were enormous and black, spun out behind the plane as smoothly as if pasted to the sky.

MARY*ELLEN***MARRY*ME?

CHAPTER

14

The marching band did not have a large repertoire.

The band director wished he could play a wedding march, or at least a waltz or a love song. But this year half the band was new, and the only thing his least-experienced flutists and clarinetists could play was "Stars and Stripes Forever."

So that was what they played.

The director lifted his arms to force their eyes on him, and away from the plane. Stepping backward, he led them marching toward Pres and Mary Ellen. Trombones hitting the bass notes and piccolos trilling the high ones, the Tarenton High School Marching Band began a parade.

Throbbing music filled the playing grounds. Every foot in every group moved to the rhythm. The Pompon Squad jumped up and down, screaming and waving pompons. It is a high risk to jump on open bleachers, but nobody worried about broken bones. They shrieked at the top of their lungs and the words were, "Say yes, Mary Ellen!"

As for the six Varsity Cheerleaders, nobody remembered a single beat of a single cheer. Making noises more like war whoops than cheers, they raced across the field. Ducking in front of the oncoming marching band, the cheerleaders sped toward Pres and Mary Ellen.

As the plane circled, the letters were turned backward to the crowd. The plane became a silver dot again, finished its enormous turn, and came back for another reading.

Ardith Engborg stared into the sky. Oh, Pres! she thought. You've played some crazy pranks, but marriage is no prank. Do you have any idea what you're doing? At nineteen?

Ardith was the only one to *walk* in Pres and Mary Ellen's direction.

Olivia was screaming and laughing and waving her arms like a windmill. She had never seen anything so romantic in her entire life. She had never *dreamed* of anything so romantic in her entire life. Imagine renting a plane to propose for you! Imagine doing this in front of the entire town and school!

Oh, it was so romantic. "Say yes, Mary Ellen!" she yelled with the rest of them. And she thought, and then ask me to be your bridesmaid!

"A cheerleader wedding!" Hope exclaimed.

"We could do it in scarlet and white," Tara

144

said. "Little megaphones for favors. Little scarlet sneakers in the bouquets. Little — "

Hope, Jessica, and Olivia gave her scathing looks.

"Tara, that is so tacky I cannot even believe you said it," Olivia informed her. Olivia was not about to have anything tacky at *this* wedding. She would help Mary Ellen choose everything. Mary Ellen had pretty good taste, but people got excited about their weddings. Olivia would have to be sure Mary Ellen didn't listen to a single thing Tara suggested. It would be embarrassing. Little megaphones? Little sneakers? Shudder. Olivia wanted a wedding in lace and satin and ivory and that was that, and there would be no interference from Tara.

"Stars and Stripes Forever" became louder and louder as the band got closer and the players got more excited. The flutists ran out of breath and regretted not taking trumpet lessons, because the trumpets were able to fill the air with their volume and the flutes were just puffing away. The bass drum and snare drum musicians were joyous because the harder they played, the happier their audience.

Ardith wished she had a video camera trained on this scene. What a film it would make! If only Tarenton High could always show this much spirit! Several hundred kids descended on Pres and Mary Ellen like a mob of fans.

Everybody was laughing.

Or screaming.

Or jumping up and down.

Except the two who mattered most.

Pres and Mary Ellen sat very still. Wrapped in one coat, they were almost a single person on the top bleacher: two blond heads, one dark coat.

And the band played on.

Pres was so proud of himself he could hardly speak.

Mary Ellen was so stunned she could hardly speak.

"Stars and Stripes Forever" blared.

"Please?" Pres whispered.

Mary Ellen struggled for breath. "We're too young."

"We're very mature."

"We're not very mature," Mary Ellen said, starting to cry. She had not expected tears. The tears felt like somebody else's, because inside she was not weeping at all. She was filled with joy. This time Pres Tilford was not joking. He was serious. He really meant it that he really wanted Mary Ellen. Forever. In good things and in bad, Pres wanted *her*.

She stared back at the plane. The banner behind it was briefly invisible as the plane changed course. She stared until she could read it again; M A R Y * E L L E N * * * M A R R Y * M E ?

The piccolos were going berserk trilling.

The bass drums were going to need new skins.

The trumpets were screaming.

Mary Ellen hardly even heard them. She never once looked down at them. He loves me, she thought. Crazy Pres can only be serious in a crazy way.

"I love you," Pres said.

"I love you, too. I always will."

But that was not an answer.

They both knew it wasn't an answer.

They didn't hear the band begin "Stars and Stripes Forever" for the third time. They didn't see Olivia hurtle past the crowds and vault up the bleachers toward them.

They saw each other.

In what felt like silence, Pres and Mary Ellen waited, trying to know each other's hearts, wanting to hear each other's words.

And Mary Ellen said, "Yes."

CHAPTER

15

"I think you should be engaged for at least a year," Mrs. Tilford said.

Pres thought that was ridiculous. "Being engaged for a week will be plenty," he informed his mother.

Mrs. Kirkwood said, "Darling, I think you should be engaged for at least a year."

Mary Ellen could not imagine waiting for a whole year. Once she said yes, she meant yes, and now she wanted the marriage to happen. "A year?" she said. "A *year*, Mother?"

Ardith Engborg gave them each a hug when she was alone with them a few days later and said, "I think you should wait at least a year."

"What is this magic stuff about a year?" demanded Pres. "What is going to happen in twelve months other than us losing our minds from being forced to wait?"

"Waiting builds character," Ardith said.

"He has plenty of character," Mary Ellen happily said. "If he had any more character, I couldn't handle him."

"Oh, so you actually think you can handle me, huh?" Pres teased.

They laughed, and kissed, and rubbed noses, and nibbled each other's ears, and hugged, and Ardith said, "I'm wrong. Marry. Quickly. So you can do this in private."

"I hear it's going to be a cheerleader wedding," a classmate said.

"What does that mean?" demanded Diana. "They'll wear their varsity uniforms down the aisle? They'll get married in the gym? They'll skip an organ playing love songs and have the cheerleading squad shouting, 'Yea, rah, rah, marriage'?"

Diana was furious.

Things had been going so well. She had managed to get the squad riled up and confused, until Olivia was on the brink of quitting. And now look at them. All soft and mushy over the love story that had fallen into their laps. All quivery about flowers and dresses and churches. A basketball game last night and Tara never even noticed Diana sitting behind her. Never had the squad been so tight. You would have thought the six of *them* were getting married. They practically held hands and kissed through the entire game.

"Enough to make anybody sick," Diana sniffed to anybody who would listen.

Diana did not realize the girls around her were looking at her in contempt rather than with interest. "Diana is the sick one," muttered one of the girls.

"Yeah. Sick with jealousy."

. . . "I hear the Tilfords are giving them the wedding for a wedding gift," Jessica said.

Patrick nodded. "Pres is their only child and I think they'd rather he waited about a decade, but since he's ready now, they're going to be ready, too. They want the wedding to be perfect."

Jessica nodded. When she had a wedding (and hers *would* be a decade off) it, too, would be perfect. But she doubted if her vision of a perfect wedding was the same as the Tilfords'. This one sounded awfully big. The entire world had been invited. Jessica did not think she even *knew* as many girls as Mary Ellen was having in her wedding party. When I get married, it will be intimate, she thought. In spite of herself, she began dreaming about weddings, seeing herself filmy in white, her groom tall and handsome, a foggy image of a male creature down some long aisle.

Patrick said nothing. He had a much clearer picture of his wedding, but he had been burned once too often mentioning it to Jessica. He would just have to stay silent and hope she didn't abandon him once she got to college. If he could only be patient like this! He'd done fine so far. Friends. They were nice, close friends and Jessica seemed happy, and he was sort of happy, in a restless kind of way. Patrick understood completely why Pres wanted to get married so fast. Why would anybody want to be patient when they could be with the person they loved instead?

Jessica seemed to think they ought to be patient until he, Patrick, was bald.

Patrick sighed. "I'm going to be best man," he told Jessica. "Avery will be an usher. And Walt Manners, who used to be on the squad, is trying to make arrangements so he can come back to be an usher, too, but we haven't heard for sure yet."

Mrs. Tilford touched the fabric of the wedding gown.

The impossibly sleek, soft, slipperiness of the satin made her want to weep. "Oh, Mary Ellen," she whispered. "It's so beautiful. You're so beautiful!"

The gown was fitted very tightly. Slender sleeves clung to Mary Ellen's graceful arms like a leotard. The neckline dipped so that the magnificent jewelry that had once belonged to Pres's grandmother could hang perfectly at Mary Ellen's throat. The seams curved sharply in at the waist and then flared out into yards of fabric. Delicate lace covered the entire top of the gown, and the little beads sewn into flowers caught the light and gleamed like a thousand prisms. When Mary Ellen breathed, the dress trembled with light.

In a hundred tucks the ivory satin fell to the floor and behind Mary Ellen, forming a six-foot train. At the base of the train, the flowery lace and bead motif was repeated.

The seamstress stood behind the bride to adjust the way the gown fell.

So young! Felicia Tilford thought, staring at her future daughter-in-law. She loved her son, and she had come to love Mary Ellen, but did these two know how hard marriage was? How difficult a task to keep those simple-sounding vows?

Touching the satin made her want to weep for the youth and innocence of it all, and pray for their happiness. She did not know when she had felt so emotional about anything. Weddings!

The baby she had cuddled and sung lullabies to was going to be a married man.

Impossible.

She and her husband were doing all they could to make the wedding perfect for Pres. After that, he would be on his own. They could buy the gown and the reception, the limousine and the flowers . . . but they could not buy peace and a happy home for these two.

Be happy! Felicia Tilford thought. "And what about a veil?" she said to Mary Ellen. "Do you want something over your face or just something coming down in back?"

Peter said, "If I hear one more syllable about the color of the bridesmaids' gowns, I am going to throw up."

Sean grinned. "I know the feeling."

"We are standing here in the Tarenton High School gymnasium and a basketball game is in progress. We are about to lose to Garrison. This is possibly the most important game of the season so far. It will decide the championship. And four out of six cheerleaders are worrying about whether their shoes were dyed the right shade of pink."

The boys rolled their eyes up.

"Look at it this way," Sean said. "It could be worse. It could be *us* getting married."

Peter stuck one finger deep into his mouth to indicate gagging. He thought better of this, and stuck all five fingers into his mouth. Sean attempted ten fingers. Peter said, "Maybe we could fit our toes in, too."

Both boys, of course, had been invited to the wedding.

While it was not in fact a cheerleader wedding, there would be quite a few cheerleaders present. The girls were trying to talk the boys into wearing their uniforms to the wedding. Peter felt the only thing worse than a wedding would be attending the wedding in sweatsuits.

"No, no," said Tara impatiently. "Not to the wedding. To the reception. We want to do cheers when they get into their car to drive away. You know how at military weddings the bride and groom walk under crossed swords? Well, all the new cheerleaders and all the old cheerleaders can stand in two lines and cheer the bride and groom along, waving their Tarenton pompons!"

"I am definitely going to be sick," Peter informed her. "Probably on your feet, Tara."

Sean said, "This is in *public* you want to do this, Tara?"

Hope caught Peter's eye and they laughed together, and she found herself hugging him. She thought, I really do like Peter.

But then, I really do like Avery.

But Avery is going back to college eventually. But. . . .

"My dears," said their coach, "it is important to know what we are wearing to the wedding, but I do not think it has to be decided in the sixth minute of the fourth quarter. It might be a fun little activity to do a few cheers. Just for a change of pace, you know."

"Angie can come!" Mary Ellen cried. Dancing in a circle in their tiny kitchen she hugged her mother and sister fiercely. "Now my wedding will be perfect!"

"Ooooh!" squealed Gemma. "We haven't seen Angie in ages and ages and ages and ages!"

"She'll be flying in at the last minute," said Mary Ellen worriedly.

"This whole wedding is pretty last-minute," her mother said. "I still wish that you and Pres would wait just a — "

"Oh, Mother," her beautiful daughter said, hugging her so hard it squashed the words she would have said. "It's not last-minute. It's just the right minute!"

Mrs. Kirkwood kissed her older child and sat down at the tiny scarred table to study her notebook. This was actually Felicia Tilford's wedding, with Mrs. Kirkwood standing by, obeying instructions. She had momentarily been angry. The mother of the bride was not having all the fun. However, the mother of the bride was not paying all the bills, either, and Mrs. Kirkwood had to admit that Mary Ellen's wedding would have been a very different thing if the Kirkwoods had covered the costs: a few close friends at home, period.

For a moment she yearned for that wedding, a wedding within her means, a wedding she and her husband gave, for their own child.

But Mary Ellen was whirling like a tornado with excitement and joy, and Mrs. Kirkwood was swept up by the emotion and by the deadlines of getting things done, and what point was there in saying anything now? She watched her daughter dance through the tiny house, dance back, and dial the number of the bridal shop to set up a last-minute fitting for Angie.

Very softly Gemma said, "Mama, don't be upset."

Mrs. Kirkwood fought tears.

"I know what you're thinking," Gemma murmured. "You wish this could be *our* wedding. But it isn't. It's Melon's. And she and Pres love to make a splash. Look at it this way: We get a free ride through the whole spectacular affair."

Mary Ellen's mother was not sure it was a good thing to start a marriage on the basis of a free ride. And yet, why not? The wedding would be beautiful, and she approved of beauty.

"Now," Gemma said practically, "we have to

decide what *you're* going to wear, Mama. Mrs. Tilford's dress is to be robin's egg blue. The bridesmaids will be in three shades of rose, with mine the deepest color. I think you could take a deep blue. Royal blue. To pick up the color of your eyes."

. It had been many years since anybody commented on Mrs. Kirkwood's eyes. It was from her that Mary Ellen had inherited those cornflower blue eyes that so entranced Pres. Mrs. Kirkwood remembered herself, twenty-five years before, at her senior prom. Her gown, taffeta and tulle. "The color of your eyes," her date whispered, kissing her. She married him a few years later. And never regretted it.

"Yes," Mary Ellen's mother said, smiling. "Yes. Cornflower blue. Let's go shopping."

"Okay," Olivia said, frowning down at her own list. "Now. Flowers, Mary Ellen. What are we doing for flowers?"

It didn't bother Mary Ellen at all that Olivia was saying "we." The wedding had become a community effort since it all had to come together so quickly, and Mary Ellen loved it. She was completely the center of every single moment. She always had at least one companion and everybody around her gave opinions — and then deferred to her.

Pres, listening to all this, was a bit astonished to find the wedding had slipped out of his hands so fast and so completely.

"Girls have weddings," his mother explained.

"It won't be much of a wedding without me," Pres protested. "And it was all my idea anyhow."

The group of women and girls around him paused and considered this. His mother, his fiancée, her mother, three bridesmaids, two aunts. . . .

"Well, that's so," his mother agreed. "What would *you* like for flowers, Pres?"

Pres could not think of a single flower except dandelions. "Uh," he said, trying to imagine a bouquet that would make him happy. He realized he did not care in the slightest what kind of bouquet Mary Ellen carried.

"How does baby's breath and white roses sound?" his bride asked.

Pres liked the idea of roses. But he was not given a chance to say so. "Too dull," Olivia put in. "Come on, Melon, you have to pick up the rose shades in our gowns. Or else have a nice, colorful contrast to them. Maybe yellow roses and — "

"*Yellow?*" Pres's Aunt Margaret repeated in dismay. "*Yellow?*"

"You don't want white because your gown is ivory, Melon," Gemma said. "White will barely show against ivory. You want color."

"Right," Olivia said. "And yellow roses would — "

"*Yellow?*" said Aunt Margaret, who obviously had a thing against yellow.

Maybe weddings *are* for girls, Pres thought. They're certainly not talking about anything I care about.

He watched Mary Ellen, hoping she would abandon flower talk and come away with him, so they could be alone together. She didn't.

I have to be patient, after all, Pres thought.

But only for a matter of days. Not that long, long year they all liked so much. Days.

Pres went for a solitary drive and mentally counted up the hours, and knew he could be patient that long.

Avery went to Hope's house for dinner only because he'd be afraid to look Dr. or Mrs. Chang in the eye if he weaseled out of the invitation at the last minute.

He envied Sean and Peter, being able to vanish from the wedding scene. Even Pres, whose wedding it was, could slip off. But he, Avery, lived in the Tilford house. Dinner conversation was exclusively wedding. Telephones were reserved for wedding calls. Guests focused solely on the wedding.

What if this wedding stuff was catching? What if he gave Hope one really good kiss (the kind of kiss he'd been fantasizing about) and she started to think wedding?

What if her mind ran down a track like this: Avery is the same age as Pres. . . . Avery is Pres's cousin. . . . Cousins are very similar. . . . I, too, could marry a Tilford.

Avery shuddered.

Any girl thinking of marriage had better think of some other boy. Avery would join the French Foreign Legion before he would get engaged. Was there still a French Foreign Legion? He would have to look into the matter. A person had to have a place to flee.

Hundreds of miles away, Angie sat in a darkening room, her mind so filled with thought she could not stir to turn on the lights. "I'm going to be a bridesmaid in Pres and Mary Ellen's wedding," she whispered to herself. "How can that be?"

One year ago, she had worn the short pleated skirt and the heavy woolen sweater of the cheerleading squad. She, Mary Ellen, Pres, Walt, Nancy, and Olivia had been an inseparable six. She had been the serious one of the crowd. If anybody could have been expected to marry young, it was Angie. And now marriage seemed the strangest, least-likely activity Angie could imagine.

She was too swept up in college. She loved every moment of college. She adored the crowds of boys who walked past her on campus, calling out her name, the boys who lived in half her dorm, and the boys in her labs and in the library. She loved the silly, sisterly fun of dorm life. She loved going to football games and singing in the concert choir and working on the campus radio station.

College was a perfect world. Give one particle of it up? For some boy who would still be there a few years later?

No. Four years of college for Angie, and she intended to get the most joy out of every day of it.

Hard to believe that Manhattan had not snapped Mary Ellen up and led her to success in modeling. Harder still to believe that Melon had come back to Tarenton — and was happy about it. And Pres, of all boys in their graduating class, was the one who was eager to get married.

Angie shook her head.

If only she could return to Tarenton a few days earlier. She would like to see the two of them together and satisfy herself that this really was right for them — that Mary Ellen and Pres were doing the right thing.

She almost dialed Mary Ellen's number.

Melon, are you doing this because now you'll be a success? New York said no, but the Tilfords said yes?

Melon, are you getting married because it will fill the time?

Melon, are you getting married because you're poor and Pres is rich, and rich is better?

Oh, Melon, do you really love each other?

But in the dark, Angie Poletti knew she would never have answers. No human being can ever really know what makes another do something.

She wanted her old crowd back, in the old way, in the old setting: the six of them and their dates, cheering and partying through Tarenton

High. But they were gone forever, and soon one of them would not even have the same last name.

Angie's roommate threw open the door, banging it against the corner of Angie's wardrobe. Turning on the light, the roomie gasped. "Angie! Why are you sitting in the dark? You scared me. Are you sick? Listen, a bunch of boys over at The Jungle are having a party. Come on. You don't want to miss it. Get up. Let's go have fun!"

Oh, Angie thought, I'm glad to be me!

And she jumped up and ran with her roommate to have fun.

Hope wished Avery would get the flu.

Not that she didn't like him.

But this wedding stuff — you could drown in it. It was delightful to play games with. But when you actually started thinking about it, thinking, So *this* is where heavy dating leads. . . . Wow. Did you ever come to the edge of panic.

Her parents' marriage was rather traditional. She would sit at home watching them function together and think, Would I do this? Would I do laundry and make up grocery lists? Would I want to be sure the tires got rotated on the car and worry about the roof leak? Would I want to eat at the same table, in the same room, with the same person for the rest of my life?

It was enough to make anybody want to practice her violin instead.

But as for Mary Ellen herself, she had no questions and she never looked back.

When she said, "Yes!" on the top bleacher to the tune of "Stars and Stripes Forever," that's what it was. Forever. She felt she had already taken her wedding vows. The wedding was a gala affair and she would be its star. But she had already said yes, and she had said it to the boy she loved.

Perhaps because it was a Tilford wedding, every aspect of planning fell easily into place. Even her gown had been refitted overnight. Now it hung in a clear plastic wrap in her closet. She was drawn to the closet as she was drawn to Pres: She had to touch it over and over, and gaze upon it, and touch it again.

My wedding gown, she thought.

I, Mary Ellen Kirkwood, am getting married. Next Saturday.

In this gown.

She held it against herself and danced in the dark.

CHAPTER

The entire backseat of the Mercedes was filled with satin and the scent of gardenias. Olivia was trembling with nervousness. Angie kept swallowing and gasping for breath and giggling.

"Now, girls," said Pres's Aunt Margaret, "stay calm. We're in the home stretch."

"Actually we're in the church stretch," Angie said.

"Right. And even if the car does break down, we're only two blocks from the church and nobody will miss the wedding."

Olivia's hands were like ice. Had she ever been this frightened? Even terribly important things like cheerleading tryouts or SAT exams hadn't made her this nervous.

"It's because of the occasion," Angie said. "Mary Ellen is the first of us to get married, stepping into a future we can't quite imagine."

Olivia didn't like thinking about the marriage part of it. She just liked the wedding part.

When I get engaged, she thought suddenly, it *will* be for a long time. We've barely had time to realize this is going to happen, and now here it is. I want to savor it. I want it to last.

She stared into the yellow of Aunt Margaret's hat: a crowd-stopping chromium yellow with a brim from shoulder to shoulder, and a dress of flowers. Margaret was all clothing and no person. Beyond the sloping hat brim, Olivia saw the church.

It was a large stone building, with a soaring roof that made Olivia think of European cathedrals. Inside, the carpets were dark blue, the pews were of dark wood, and the stained glass was Victorian red and green and gold.

The wedding party would look so soft and lovely against that background!

Olivia counted two Jaguars, a Volvo, a little crowd of BMW's, and four Mercedes. Two sleek limousines were closest to the steps. The bride had arrived ahead of her maids.

The sky was gray. It was chilly, but not wintry. Against the stone and the gray sky and the grass not yet green, the guests in their bright spring suits were as colorful as tulips and daffodils. We're celebrating, Olivia thought. She began laughing from excitement.

Angie said wistfully, "I wish we could have ridden in the limousine."

Avery Tilford, wearing a black jacket with black satin trim and a black cummerbund, black shoes shining like rainbow coal, opened the door for Angie. "Well, at least I can be a gentleman and let you out of your Mercedes," he said. The girls emerged slowly, adjusting their enormous skirts, and letting the satin swish into place. Olivia had never thought of Avery as handsome, but he was, in that suit. All the men looked so dashing! She had never realized how dress clothing for men could change them. Avery moved with an adult grace, and when he inclined his head toward her, Olivia felt like a princess.

If *I* feel like royalty, she thought, how is Mary Ellen feeling?

The guests cried out, "How lovely you look, girls! What a perfect color. I love those gowns."

Olivia took the shallow stone steps carefully, lifting the hem of the long skirt and wishing she could wear clothes like this every day. With each step the tiny satin slippers peeked out.

She led Angie to the bride's room.

Laughing girls filled it to overflowing, the photographer was sliding in between them, Mrs. Tilford was giving out last-minute instructions, Mrs. Kirkwood was crying, and Mary Ellen —

Oh, Mary Ellen looked like an angel.

Her hair was woven into tiny braids that encircled her elegant face. Resting on the curves of braid was a circlet of flowers: tiny, white, and graceful. A gossamer veil cascaded down from the flowers and flowed over Mary Ellen's shoulders and down her back as if it were hair, too — Rapunzel's hair, so long, so ethereally beautiful.

Mary Ellen was neither speaking nor smiling;

165

she was simply radiant. Her eyes rested on each of the girls and sparkled and went back into a place where only Mary Ellen was: a daydream about to come true.

Gemma, the maid of honor, looked serene and proud. Her hair fell simply and her circlet of flowers was pink and not white, and no veil fell from it.

In the long gilt-framed mirror that hung on one wall of the bride's room, Olivia stole a glance at herself. She and the other seven bridesmaids, dressed in their rose red satin, were all, each one of them, beautiful. Even I am beautiful, Olivia thought. Little me. Not stunning like Mary Ellen nor sweet like Angie, but special, like a pixie who just landed.

Someone handed Olivia her bouquet and she clung to the fat handle and smelled the sweet scent. Mary Ellen seemed dazed, and Olivia could think of nothing to say to her anyhow, so she simply smiled on. Oh, Melon! Olivia thought. *Be happy.*

They were all telling her to be happy.

Mary Ellen was touched but she was also surprised. How could she be anything but happy? Who on earth could ever have more than she had on this day?

I'm glad it went so fast, she thought. It isn't the dating I want, or the game-playing, or the wedding plans. It's Pres. I want him forever.

I want to be "us."

The room seemed oddly blurry, as if the old

166

life was slipping out of focus and the new life had not yet begun so she could see it clearly.

"Are you all right, darling?" her mother asked anxiously.

Mary Ellen kissed her mother. "Oh, yes," she said. "I'm perfect."

The ushers — Avery, Sean, and the rest — had things to do and schedules to follow, guests to seat and boutonnieres to distribute. Pres and Patrick waited in a little hall back behind the choir loft, getting more and more nervous every moment.

Walt and Nancy had not been able to come after all. Nancy, who'd been swamped by exams, sent Mary Ellen a note full of best wishes. And a letter from Walt had been delivered at the very last minute to Pres. IT'S NOT TOO LATE! Walt wrote in block letters, to be sure Pres didn't miss the message. YOU WANT TO VISIT ME FOR A FEW YEARS AND REGAIN YOUR SANITY?

It seemed wiser not to relay Walt's wedding message to Mary Ellen. When Pres talked to her that morning on the phone, he said yes, he would be there, and no, he would not leave her standing at the altar, and yes, he still loved her very much.

Now he was beginning to feel the edge of panic.

"Who am I kidding?" he said to Patrick. "I'm feeling a *lot* of panic."

Patrick wasn't feeling too relaxed himself. They could hear the organ playing. The music that had seemed so cheery and charming last night at rehearsal now sounded ominous and dark. "It's a short service," said Patrick. "The whole thing will be over in no time." For the nine hundredth time he felt to be sure he had the wedding rings in his pocket.

The minister popped in a side door, startling both boys badly. "Now, now," he said, grinning. "Let's not bolt just because the door opens. We've got about thirty seconds. You both follow me. We stand to the right of the altar. Face down the aisle and wait for the processional."

Thirty seconds.

Walt's words typed their way through Pres's mind.

He was having a hard time catching his breath.

Patrick's fingers were locked around the two rings.

The bright clarion tones of the trumpet filled the church.

"Hands out of your pockets," the minister said sternly to Patrick. "All right. This is our cue. March."

Patrick wished he hadn't said *march* quite so authoritatively. It sounded like an execution that way.

But the black robes swished out the door.

And Pres and Patrick marched.

The weak wintery sun could not penetrate the deep-set windows of the old stone church. Candles in sconces were lit along the walls, and white flowers in trailing ribbons were hung on the end of each pew. Under two enormous bouquets of pink and white flowers lay a magnificently embroidered white altar cloth.

Pres looked briefly into the congregation. But the march was beginning, and the faces turned away from him and peered down the aisle to see the bride.

Well, Walt, Pres thought, I think it's too late to regain my sanity now.

The ushers walked down the side aisle and joined them. He felt marginally better with a platoon of friends spread out at his side.

The silvery melody of the trumpet matched the rhythm of Pres's wildly beating heart.

Olivia was the first bridesmaid.

She came down the aisle with the slow pace calculated to make it last longer. Pres would have preferred to see her run up like a cheerleader and get the show on the road.

He glanced at his mother. She caught his eye and smiled at him.

The second bridesmaid came, and the third, and then in the wide stone arch at the rear of the sanctuary, Pres could see Mr. Kirkwood and a slim white-sleeved arm hooked in his.

First he saw the dress: a great fall of glistening ivory that cascaded across the dark carpet. Two more bridesmaids moved gracefully down the aisle, then Gemma, and then at last he could see Mary Ellen.

It did not look like a wedding to him, but a Christmas pageant. Mary Ellen had been the angel as far back as first grade, when even then she had been the star of Tarenton.

My angel now, Pres thought. He was laughing, and the nerves left him, and he forgot Patrick and the rings and the congregation and the silver trumpet.

He saw only Mary Ellen.

The usher had asked Ardith Engborg whether she was a friend of the bride or the groom. "Both," she told him. The usher paused in seating her and explained he needed to know which side of the church she wanted to sit on. "I want to straddle the aisle," she told him. He looked shocked. "I'm only kidding," Ardith said. "Put me on the groom's side, then. I'm more surprised by the groom than by the bride. He's the one I want to keep my eye on."

Now the usher was truly nervous. He seated Ardith quickly and abandoned her.

Now she sat listening to the vows. Pres's voice rang clear and happy. Mary Ellen's trembled. The congregation were all smiling, as if they too had just fallen in love.

My best cheerleaders, Ardith thought.

Who would ever have thought, with all that those six went through, that we would ever have a cheerleader wedding?

Her eyes filled with tears.

Gemma took Mary Ellen's bouquet for her and balanced her own flowers as well as her sister's. Mary Ellen took Pres's hand and Mr. Kirkwood returned to his pew to sit with his wife.

The minister had showed them several different versions of the ceremony, but Mary Ellen had chosen the most traditional of all. The words that had wed couples for centuries were the words she wanted. Gemma, listening to the cadences of the vows, never took her eyes off her sister.

The minister looked at Pres. "Preston? Wilt thou have this woman to be thy wedded wife? To have and to hold from this day forth?"

Gemma closed her eyes.

"I will," Pres said.

It was really happening. In a moment, she would have a married sister.

The satin that wrapped her, the tiny beads that glistened, the lace that trembled, the veil whose soft weight she could feel on her shoulders — Mary Ellen felt like the illustration of every fairy tale she had ever read.

I am the most beautiful woman on earth, she thought.

Pres's hand held hers tightly and she held his back. They kept looking at the minister, and then back to each other, and then half laughing with delight.

The prayers ended.

The minister pronounced a benediction. "The Lord bless you and keep you. The Lord make his face to shine upon you. . . ."

Their faces shone upon each other.

"Amen," said the minister.

It was done.

They were married.

She thought, *I am Mary Ellen Kirkwood Tilford*.

The minister said, "Pres, you may kiss your wife."

CHAPTER

The sun was out as the bride and groom left the church, and the laughter, the honking horns, the clanking soda cans on the back of Pres's car, the church bells chiming — the entire world that mattered to Pres and Mary Ellen was celebrating as noisily and happily as it could.

The mood of elegance lasted but an hour: The satin and lace, the rose and the ivory, might almost have been left behind in the church.

For the reception was a cheerleader reception.

The country club was transformed into one great scarlet and white display. White cloths with scarlet runners decorated the tables, and between the candles lay the tiny scarlet megaphones Tara had suggested, each tilted up to make a vase, holding white carnations. Enormous blowup photographs of Pres and Mary Ellen as Varsity Cheerleaders covered one wall. Scarlet and white pompons sewn together into a great horseshoe made a spectacular entryway where each group of guests paused for photographs.

The band was a group that had graduated from Tarenton about four years earlier, and they played exclusively from a list of hits that Pres and Mary Ellen had given them. Percussion throbbed beneath every conversation, and the room literally shook with excitement.

The reception line moved slowly. Mary Ellen had never hugged so many people in her life.

And if some of the adult and out-of-town guests were astonished when the band suddenly played "Stars and Stripes Forever" none of the kids were!

The dinner was excellent, or so Mary Ellen was told. She could not eat a bite. She was too busy laughing and hugging and kissing and laughing some more.

The dancing began.

Mary Ellen had danced many a dance with Pres, but never had she been the first on the floor, with her husband's arm at her waist. She wanted to shout a cheer at the top of her lungs: Look at me! Look who I am! Look what I'm doing!

But she didn't need to tell them; they were all looking. And she didn't need to lead a cheer; they cheered on their own. And then the whole room was dancing. Pres circled the floor with his new mother-in-law, and Gemma danced with Mr. Tilford. Avery danced with Hope's mother and Olivia danced with somebody's twelve-year-old cousin. Mary Ellen danced with Pres's eighty-three-year-old great-uncle, and Sean danced with Mary Ellen's second cousin Marissa.

"Do you think it's time yet?" Tara said to Olivia under the cover of the pounding band.

Olivia, between partners, paused to check her watch. "We don't want to do it too soon."

"But we risk not being able to do it at all," Tara protested. "What if Mary Ellen and Pres decide to leave early?"

Olivia could not imagine anybody leaving this fabulous party early, and certainly not the bride and groom. But perhaps they would rather leave for their honeymoon than dance the night away. Who knew?

Olivia and Tara walked past the tables where the gifts were on display. About half had not yet been opened, and their wrappings and bows were just as lovely as the ones that had been opened: crystal and china, silver and pottery, linens and picture frames, lamps and cookware, porcelain and clocks.

"Where are they going on their honeymoon?" Tara asked.

Olivia shook her head. "Mary Ellen won't tell me. I just hope it's someplace romantic. Paris or London or Rome."

In fact, it was Hawaii.

Mary Ellen had had a wonderful time buying clothes and luggage for the trip. "Why do you need all those clothes?" Pres wanted to know. "We'll be on the beach. Just bring a change of bikinis." Which just went to show what men knew.

For only the fourth time in an evening of solid dancing, Mary Ellen and Pres were partners. It was a slow dance and she leaned on Pres and he said to her, "So, Mrs. Tilford. How are your feet holding up?"

She loved him calling her that. "These feet could dance forever," she told him dreamily.

"Can't. We have a plane to catch."

Mary Ellen could not believe it. Time to leave? Could her wedding actually be over already? How could it have finished so fast?

"Something funny is going on," Pres said. "There's nobody our age left in this entire room."

"If they're off trying to soap your car," Mary Ellen said, "it doesn't matter, since we're going in the limousine." Her eyes were closed and she was following Pres entirely, not wanting to make the slightest effort. Just to be there, the music in her bones, knowing it was her moment, was enough. She listened to her dress rustle and felt the slippery softness of it against her and dreamed of love.

But it isn't a dream anymore, she thought. I have it.

The band stopped in midnumber.

Mary Ellen opened her eyes and looked around.

From the opposite end of the ballroom came a pounding of feet, a clapping of hands, and a great whistling and yelling. It was a sound very familiar to Pres and Mary Ellen: the war whoops of the squad just before they started cheering in front of the crowd.

Fourteen cheerleaders in varsity uniforms came tumbling, running, and screaming through the crowd of guests. The astonished guests moved apart to give them room.

Cheerleaders who had been on the squad when Mary Ellen was a freshman! Angie and Olivia, out of their bridesmaids' gowns and into their scarlet and white skirts and sweaters! Jessica, the gymnast, tumbling in front! Five girls in a row doing cartwheels! Two boys who had graduated three years ago, lifting Hope in the air!

They reached the bride and groom.

Laughing hysterically, they did three high school cheers — substituting "Mary Ellen and Pres" for "Tarenton"! They finished up with a high-kicking routine that nobody had had time to practice — so the kicks were terrific from the cheerleaders who were still in shape, and pretty far off from the rest!

And then they formed a square, and Olivia and Tara leaped out in front and faced the guests instead of Pres and Mary Ellen.

"Give me an L!" screamed the two girls.

There was a fractional pause and then the guests said a little tentatively, "L!"

"Let's have an O!" screamed the girls.

Now they were braver. "O!" they cried.

"Let's have a V!" shrieked Tara and Olivia.

"V!" the crowd screamed.

"Let's have an E!"

"E!" they shouted.

"What does it spell?"

"Love!"

177

"Say it again?"

"Love!"

"Say it louder!"

"LOVE!"

The wedding was over.

The reception went on, but the bride and groom were gone. A married couple, on their own.

Gemma had caught the bouquet.

"It went perfectly," Olivia said contentedly.

Gemma nodded. "I loved it when you guys came out cheering. I didn't know a single thing about that. You really kept it a secret. Olivia, you're such a wonderful captain! You must have spent hours and hours on the phone finding all those cheerleaders, and getting them uniforms, and practicing with them, and pulling that act off! You can really be proud of yourself. It was the perfect cheerleader ending for the perfect cheerleader wedding."

Olivia said nothing. She had been many things this year, but not a great captain. Oh, to be able to take credit for what had happened tonight! It took all her strength of character to turn and smile at Tara, and speak up. "It was entirely Tara's idea," said Olivia. "She did all the planning and all the rehearsing."

Olivia and Tara and Gemma stood in a tiny triangle, and suddenly, as if this move, too, had been practiced each day after school, they hugged.

"Thank you, Tara," whispered Gemma, for her sister.

"Thank you, Tara," Olivia said.

But it was Tara who was happiest. She had done all that quiet work to prove that she *could* be a captain, and she had proved it. Without any slippery dealings from Diana behind her, Tara had made her point. How glad she was that there were more weeks in the school year! How happy she was to be a kid who had school and practice on Monday, instead of a honeymoon!

And Olivia knew that she had another chance to be a good captain, and that stepping aside for Tara to be the star was best for both of them.

"Tara," she said softly, "are we friends?"

There was history in that question — months of anger and annoyance and scheming. Olivia's hand rested in friendship on Tara's shoulder, and she really was not entirely sure what the answer would be.

But Tara, like another cheerleader that day, said yes, and meant it.

The band kept playing.

The kids took over the dance floor, some in dressy dresses, some in suits — and fourteen in cheerleading uniforms. They danced to rock and they danced hard, their energy pushing the adults right out of the ballroom and into the lounge as they danced on.

Pres and Mary Ellen had made a good decision, but for the rest, such decisions were far in the future.

The joy of being young and being free kept them dancing till dawn.

Who is the girl who is knocking Sean off his feet?
Read Cheerleaders #31, SHOWING OFF.

The Stepsisters

#1

The War Between the Sisters

by Tina Oaks

Chapter Excerpt

Paige Whitman unzipped the plastic cover that held the dress she was to wear to her father's wedding. She had put off looking at the dress until the very last minute. When she learned the dress would be pink, she had groaned. There were colors she loved, colors she could take or leave alone, and then there was pink, which hated her as much as she hated it!

And the style was as impossible for her as the color. She didn't even have to try the dress on to know how it would look. At sixteen she was taller than most of her friends, and thinner without being really skinny. But taller meant longer, and she knew her neck was too long to wear a low, rounded neckline like that.

Paige's instinct was to wail. Dresses were supposed to do things *for* you, not *to* you. The only tiny comforting thing she could think of was that Katie Summer Guthrie, her fifteen-year-old stepsister-to-be would be wearing a matching monstrosity. Even though pink was a blonde's color, not even Katie could look like anything in *that* dress. It was comforting that she wouldn't be alone in her humiliation.

Beyond the other bed in the hotel room they shared, Paige's ten-year-old sister Megan hummed happily as she put on her own dress. Megan was a naturally happy-go-lucky girl, but Paige had never seen her as excited as she had been since their father announced his coming marriage to Virginia Mae Guthrie. Her father had tried to control his own excitement and tell them about his bride-to-be in a calm, sensible way. But Paige knew him too well to be fooled, and anyway he gave himself dead away!

He started by telling them how he had met Virginia Mae on a business trip to Atlanta, then how beautiful she was. He went from that to her divorce five years before and how she had been raising her three children alone ever since. Paige almost giggled. Here was William Whitman, whose logic and cool courtroom delivery were legendary in Philadelphia legal circles. Yet he was jumping around from one subject to another as he talked about Virginia Mae.

Paige had driven down to Atlanta with her father and Megan earlier in the summer so the children could meet. Paige had agreed that Virginia Mae Guthrie was as lovely as she was gentle.

Paige had tried to shrug away the twinge of resentment that came when she thought of Katie Summer. The girl had to be putting on an act. *Nobody* could possibly be as lighthearted and happy as she pretended to be. And nobody would be that pretty in a fair world. Seventeen-year-old Tucker seemed like a nice enough guy, although his exaggerated good manners threw Paige off a little. Ten-year-old Mary Emily was cute. But it was awkward to be the only one holding back when her father and Megan were both so obviously deliriously happy.

Her father made the marriage plans sound so simple: "Right after our wedding, Virginia and the children will move up here to Philadelphia. We'll all be one big happy family together."

Paige had said nothing then or since, but concealing her doubts hadn't made them go away. She hated feeling like a sixteen-year-old grouch, but it just didn't make sense that everything would work out that easily. Not only would there be more than twice as many people in the same house as before, but the people themselves would be different.

Even if people from the south didn't think differently than people from the north, they certainly *sounded* different when they talked. And the Guthries were as completely southern as Paige's family was northern. Mrs. Guthrie and her three children had lived in Atlanta all their lives.

Megan giggled and fluffed out her full skirt. "Isn't it great? I can't wait to show this dress back home."

Back home. Philadelphia meant only one person to Paige . . . Jake Carson. She shuddered at the thought of Jake seeing her in that pink dress. She would die, just simply die where she stood, if he ever saw her looking this gross.

She sighed and fiddled with the neck of the pink dress, wishing she hadn't even thought of Jake. Simply running his name through her mind was enough to sweep her with those familiar waves of almost physical pain. It didn't make sense that loving anyone could be so painful. But just the memory of his face, his intense expression, the brooding darkness of his thoughtful eyes was enough to destroy her self-control.

But even when Jake looked at her, he was absolutely blind to who she really was. She knew what he thought: that she was a nice kid, that she was fun to talk to, that she was William Whitman's daughter. Period. He didn't give the slightest indication that he even realized that she was a girl, much less a girl who loved him with such an aching passion that she couldn't meet his eyes for fear he might read her feelings there.

Megan caught Paige around the waist and clung to her. "Sometimes I get scared, thinking about the changes. It *is* going to be wonderful, isn't it, Paige?" Megan's voice held the first tremulous note of doubt Paige had heard from her sister.

"Absolutely wonderful," Paige assured her, wishing she felt as much confidence as she put into her tone.

Even as she spoke, she saw Jake's face again, his dark eyes intent on hers as he had talked to her about the wedding. "Look at your dad," Jake had said. "Anything that makes him that happy has to be a lucky break for all of you."

She had nodded, more conscious of how lucky she was to be with Jake than anything else.

Jake had worked around their house in Philadelphia for about a year and a half. Paige didn't believe in love at first sight, but it had almost been that way with her. From the first day, she found herself waiting breathlessly for the next time he came to work. She found herself remembering every word he said to her, turning them over and over in her mind later. It wasn't that he was mysterious. It was more that she always had the sense of there being so much more in his mind than he was saying. She was curious about him, his life, his friends, how he thought about things. In contrast to a lot of people who smiled easily and laughed or hummed when they worked, he was silent and withdrawn unless he was talking with someone.

Before he came, she hadn't realized how painful it was to love someone the way she did Jake. She hadn't asked to fall in love with him or anybody. She had even tried desperately to convince herself that he wasn't different from other boys, just nicer and older. That didn't work because it wasn't true. Jake really was different from the boys she knew at school. Although he talked enough when he had something to say, he was mostly a little aloof without being awkward and shy. And he wasn't an ordinary kind of handsome. His features were strong, with firm cheekbones; deeply set eyes; and a full, serious mouth.

Maybe one day she would quit loving him as quickly as she had begun. But even thinking about that happening brought a quick thump of panic in her chest. Knowing how it felt to be so much in love, how could she bear to live without it?

Later, when the wedding march began and the doors of the little chapel were opened, Paige was overwhelmed with the strange feeling that she was watching all this from a distance. Even as she walked beside Katie Summer and kept careful time to the music, she didn't feel as if she was a part of what was happening.

Paige felt a touch against her arm and looked over at Katie Summer. Katie flashed her a quick, sly smile that brought a fleeting dimple to her cheek. Paige swallowed hard, ducked her head, and looked away. Later she would have to deal with this girl, but not now, not while her father was repeating the same vows he had made so many years before to her own mother.

But that quick glance had been enough to remind her of how wrong she had been about how Katie Summer would look in her matching pink dress. It made Paige feel leggy and graceless beside her.

All the Guthries were good-looking. Tucker was almost as tall as Paige's father, and comfortingly nice to look at in a different, curly-haired way. Mary Emily, behind with Megan, was button cute. But the girl at Paige's side was just too much! Katie's thick, dark blonde curls spilled in glorious profusion around her glowing face.

Her pink dress picked up the rosiness of her deep tan and showed off the sparkle of her laughing blue eyes. Paige held her head high, fighting a sudden feeling of inadequacy that made her breath come short.

Looking back, Paige was sure that the wedding brunch was as beautiful as any meal she would ever eat. As they ate, Grandma Summer bent to Paige to make conversation, her soft voice rising in an exciting, different rhythm. "Virginia Mae tells me you play the piano, Paige, and that you're an excellent student. My, I know your father is just *so* proud of you."

Before Paige could reply, Katie flipped her glowing head of curls, turned away, and put her hand on Paige's father's arm. "I just had a perfectly *terrifying* thought," she said, looking up into his face. "My goodness, I hope you don't expect *me* to have a lot of talent or be a bookworm. I've got to tell you right off that I don't believe in all that."

After an astonished look, Paige's father covered Katie's hand with his, and chuckled. "That's pretty interesting," he said. "What *do* you believe in, Katie Summer?"

Her laugh was quick and soft. "Having a *wonderful* time, just like I am today."

Naturally he beamed at her. Who could help it when everything she said sounded so intimate and appealing in that soft, coaxing drawl? Paige felt a shiver of icy jealousy. That Katie Summer was something else!